GOING, GOING ... *GONE*.

"It's just like a good auction," Clara said. "You're all enemies while it's going on, but in the end, you're all friends again . . . What happened to your clothes? You've got grass stains."

Molly was just opening her mouth to tell her mother about the appalling behavior of George-Bradley when a cry of "Help!" from behind one of the pottery tables rose above the noise.

Molly craned her head to see that the man whose name was on the tip of her tongue was lying facedown in the grass. Next to his outstretched hand lay the devil face jug, the one he had snatched away just moments before from the petite woman.

Clara drew in a sharp breath, taking in the scene.

"Thank God!" Clara exhaled the words, her eyes glued on the pottery jug where it rested on the grass. "It didn't break."

A Killer Collection

J. B. STANLEY

BERKLEY PRIME CRIME, NEW YORK

THE BERKLEY PUBLISHING GROUP
Published by the Penguin Group
Penguin Group (USA) Inc.
375 Hudson Street, New York, New York 10014, USA
Penguin Group (Canada), 90 Eglinton Avenue East, Suite 700, Toronto, Ontario M4P 2Y3, Canada
(a division of Pearson Penguin Canada Inc.)
Penguin Books Ltd., 80 Strand, London WC2R 0RL, England
Penguin Group Ireland, 25 St. Stephen's Green, Dublin 2, Ireland (a division of Penguin Books Ltd.)
Penguin Group (Australia), 250 Camberwell Road, Camberwell, Victoria 3124, Australia
(a division of Pearson Australia Group Pty. Ltd.)
Penguin Books India Pvt. Ltd., 11 Community Centre, Panchsheel Park, New Delhi—110 017, India
Penguin Group (NZ), Cnr. Airborne and Rosedale Roads, Albany, Auckland 1310, New Zealand
(a division of Pearson New Zealand Ltd.)
Penguin Books (South Africa) (Pty.) Ltd., 24 Sturdee Avenue, Rosebank, Johannesburg 2196,
South Africa

Penguin Books Ltd., Registered Offices: 80 Strand, London WC2R 0RL, England

This is a work of fiction. Names, characters, places, and incidents either are the product of the author's imagination or are used fictitiously, and any resemblance to actual persons, living or dead, business establishments, events, or locales is entirely coincidental. The publisher does not have any control over and does not assume any responsibility for author or third-party websites or their content.

A KILLER COLLECTION

A Berkley Prime Crime Book / published by arrangement with the author

PRINTING HISTORY
Berkley Prime Crime mass-market edition / January 2006

Copyright © 2006 by Jennifer Stanley.
Cover illustration by Mary Ann Lasher.
Cover design by Erica Tricarico.
Jug photos courtesy of Leland Little Auction and Estate Sales.
Interior text design by Kristin del Rosario.

ISBN: 0-425-20745-5

BERKLEY® PRIME CRIME
Berkley Prime Crime Books are published by The Berkley Publishing Group,
a division of Penguin Group (USA) Inc.,
375 Hudson Street, New York, New York 10014.
The name BERKLEY PRIME CRIME and the BERKLEY PRIME CRIME design
are trademarks belonging to Penguin Group (USA) Inc.

PRINTED IN THE UNITED STATES OF AMERICA

10 9 8 7 6 5 4 3 2 1

For my La Mama,
A true "one of a kind"

ACKNOWLEDGMENTS

I would like to thank Holly Stauffer, Anne Briggs, and Pamala Briggs for their valuable preliminary readings. You are my magical triumvirate and I couldn't have gotten this far without you. Thanks to my wonderful agent, Jessica Faust of BookEnds, Inc. who took a chance and jumped off the diving board with me. I'd also like to express my ineffable gratitude to my editor, Samantha Mandor, for being the champion of my writing. I was so lucky to have been chosen by you. Lastly, I have to praise my family for being such incredible fans.

This book would never have come to be without the inspiration I have drawn from the southern potter. The wares that I mention in *A Killer Collection* all exist in their resplendent beauty, with the exception of Jack Graham's, as he is solely a figment of my imagination. Also, the character of Sam Chance is, in real life, a North Carolina potter named Sid Luck. One can find examples of traditional southern potteries from Georgia to Virginia, and many potters still create their wares exactly as their ancestors did over a hundred years ago. To learn more about discovering southern pottery, especially in the Seagrove area of North Carolina, kindly visit www.jbstanley.com.

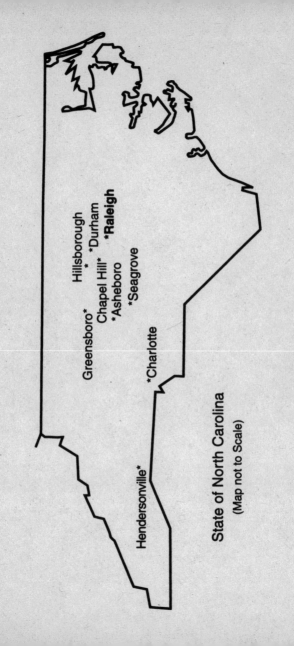

Hillsborough
*
*Durham
*Raleigh
Greensboro*
Chapel Hill*
*Asheboro
*Seagrove

*Charlotte

Hendersonville*

State of North Carolina
(Map not to Scale)

Potters have always described the forms they produce in terms of the human body. Pots have feet, bellies, shoulders, necks, and lips. Kilns are also considered anthropomorphic beings, with faces and breasts, eyes and backbones, and unpredictable behavioral patterns. Early potters keep an old pot or some totemic object on the kiln to placate its spirit.

—Nancy Sweezy, from *Raised in Clay*

The potter's hands were wide with short, thick fingers, gnarled and cracked from a lifetime of work. Small burn scars crisscrossed the tough skin on the palms from feeding wood into the kiln. Dried clay was wedged beneath the ragged fingernails. Specks of it dotted the potter's apron and stuck like gray flies to his muscular forearms.

He reached under the cloth and drew out a ball of brown clay, looking it over for any signs of obvious impurities. He placed it on the scale and removed a few chunks from the ball until the scale read five pounds. He lumped the leftovers together and returned them to their shelter to wait under the wet cloth.

Slapping the ball on his wheel so that it would hold fast and create the right amount of suction, he dipped his fingers in a pail of cloudy water and drizzled it over the expectant clay. He began pumping the foot pedal on the wheel, and as it spun around, he moistened the clay until it became malleable beneath his hands.

As the potter centered the bulk, it lurched a bit, like a drunk, and then rose upwards like a giraffe craning its neck to reach a higher branch. The wheel hummed softly as the potter worked under the light of a single bulb with the sounds of bluegrass music on the radio.

The clay was alive. Warm below his arms, it moved, stretched, and twisted. He cupped his fingers around its body, forcing the ripples to grow upward in a steady, curving shape. He pressed more firmly at the base, and hips seemed to grow as the weight of the clay settled onto itself. Around the rim, the potter pinched with one hand and smoothed the swelling sides with the other. Then, he let the pace of the wheel slow as he curled his hand around the neck of clay, pushing it upward in a gentle choking motion until it was a symmetrical spout, obedient to his will.

With a knife, he cut off the extra piece of neck and smoothed the insides of the opening. He stepped back and examined the piece, looking at the base, the round sides, and back up to the top where the centered spout emerged in perfect lines.

Satisfied, he slid a piece of wire beneath the jug and moved it gingerly onto a stone slab where it would dry. This one would not get a face. It was too late in the evening and the potter was tired. He had made enough for one day.

As he switched off the radio, he noticed the little lump of leftover clay peeking out from beneath the damp cloth. A new wedge awaited him tomorrow, and he didn't really want to unwrap the whole thing just to save this small bit. Still, he hated to waste a piece of clay. He paused, picked it up, held it, thinking.

His hands moved over it, hesitating. They weren't sure

what they were supposed to do. Without the wheel, things were uncertain. Pieces could become anything, imperfect, different.

The potter smoothed the lump into a rounded body, then pushed up a thick neck with one hand and widened the head with the other. He pinched out two long, rounded ears, and pulled forward a small nose and cheeks. Dipping his hands into the water, he smoothed the body and pushed out a swollen hump to become the back and the hind leg, then pulled out two long, identical front legs from the clay below the head. With a wooden carving stick, he traced an upright cottontail on the base of the back leg, drew paws into the little feet, and made a triangular nose, winking eyes, a grinning mouth, and six whiskers. Lastly, he carved his initials and a number onto the base.

The potter smiled, flicking away any flecks of clay from around the last piece of work he would do that night. He hid it far back behind the other taller pieces where it could remain a surprise until the moment was right.

The rabbit smiled back at him, sharing his secret among the crocks and churns, the pitchers and bowls, and the face jugs with their rows of crooked teeth. It waited for the time when the potter's hands would reach out with his brush and glaze its naked body into a cobalt the color of the deep sea. The clay was patient. It had waited hundreds of years to be formed; it could wait a little longer to be burned blue by the kiln fire.

It waited. But the gentle hands of its creator would never come again.

Chapter 1

It was quick, it was ruthless, it was in-your-face collecting. . . .
Did people really go this crazy over pottery?

—ANDREW GLASGOW, FROM *CATAWBA CLAY:*
CONTEMPORARY SOUTHERN FACE JUG MAKERS

"Time to get up!"
    The call seeped into the dark bedroom and murmured around antique woven coverlets and a turn-of-the-century walnut blanket chest. It stared at the Dutch girl with the metal bucket in her oil painting of snow, reflected the sheen on the porcelain curls of a pair Staffordshire dogs, and tickled the ecru page corners on a stack of leather-bound books. Finding no response, it accepted defeat and melted into the open mouth of a large cherry corner cupboard filled with row upon row of white-glazed pottery glowing with life in the weak, first stripes of dawn light.

    "MADAM!" This call was loud enough to stir the silence of the room and awaken the sleeping woman. The gray tabby beside her burrowed a sharp claw into the woman's hand as punishment for daring to move a body part.

    The door was flung open without ceremony and a rectangle of light from the kitchen burst into the room like an uninvited guest.

"Who do you have in there?" Molly's mother asked from the doorframe, and without waiting for an answer, asked the groggy feline, "Sophie, would you like some milk?"

The rotund tabby turned toward the voice and issued a small chirp of assent. Molly, whose nickname was "Madam" in her mother's house, turned over and buried her head beneath the pillow.

In the kitchen, her mother sang little ditties to her seven felines, cracked open cans, and distributed dry food into bowls. Cats meowed, fridge and cupboard doors were opened and closed, the microwave whirred and beeped. Then her mother was back, balancing something carefully in one hand and turning on the lamp with the other.

"Get up, Molly. It's time to go."

"I'm up, I'm up. What time is it?"

"4:45."

"Four! This is insane, Ma." Molly sat up and pushed a strand of dark hair out of her face. "You are truly an evil woman," she mumbled.

"Get up. Sophie wants her milk, and she doesn't like anyone on the bed when she's eating."

Molly looked at the porcelain doll-sized teacup and saucer her mother held with as much disdain as she could muster. Sophie glared accusingly at her in return.

"I hope you realize that I am going to be crabby all day," Molly announced as she shuffled off to the bathroom.

"Yes, dear. But I'm used to you."

"Hrmphh."

* * *

It was a cool, predawn morning. Molly shivered and wiped the condensation from the car windshield. Beneath fading stars, she watched as her mother loaded some rubber bins stuffed with bubble wrap into the trunk. It was hard to believe that this was the beginning of what would become another stiflingly hot June day in North Carolina. Molly rubbed the goose bumps on her arms and climbed into the driver's seat of her mother's pearl-white Lexus.

By 5:30, they were merging onto interstate 85 South, toward Seagrove, home of the southern potters. As Molly sipped her warm sweet coffee, her mother offered her a banana. Molly crossly waved it away.

"I can't eat at this hour, Ma. The truckers are the only people crazy enough to be out, and they're probably getting paid much more than I am."

"The *other* collectors are out here too."

"Oh," Molly moaned, ignoring her mother, "I wish I hadn't volunteered to cover these pottery fair things. I *hate* getting up when it's still dark out."

"They're called kiln openings. And once you've been to one, you'll be hooked for life. I know you!"

"Well, it was your idea to suggest these articles to *Collector's Weekly,* and now I'm driving instead of sleeping. My editor thinks a series on pottery is a great idea, and he never likes anything."

Her mother examined a minute stain on her teal cardigan sweater. "The collecting world needs to be educated about southern potters, and you're just the person to do it."

Molly had been an English teacher at an exclusive private school for eight years when the job started to wear on her. Though people assumed most teachers worked a short day and took summers off, Molly worked long days, graded papers on weekends, and spent every summer teaching extra classes in order to meet her mortgage payments. After eight years, she felt that she had no time for herself.

Whenever she did have a few moments to spare, she spent them attending auctions and browsing antique shops. Soon she was submitting articles to *Collector's Weekly* for extra spending money, and when a full-time staff position became available, she jumped at the chance to get paid for doing what she loved most.

She typically wrote on the bigger-name antique auctions in her area, driving around Virginia, North Carolina, and South Carolina to snap pictures and to interview auctioneers and bidders. Her articles featured detailed descriptions of the items that brought in the highest prices and quotes from satisfied buyers.

After covering the auction beat for a year, she noticed that more and more southern pottery was appearing at auction and then disappearing at exorbitant prices. Knowing little about the subject, she asked her mother for a quick course on the world of southern pottery.

She had received a pile of books to read, but her mother warned her that the written word could never compete with the real thing. Molly would have to meet the potters and see them working in person to fully understand why people went wild over their ware.

Molly's mother, Clara Appleby, had once owned a thriving antique shop. After a while, she discovered that she hated being tied down to retail hours and dealing with finicky customers, so she switched her business to become a dealer in southern folk art pottery. Instead of renting and maintaining a costly shop space, she now conducted business using a simple Web site and a "shop" located in the log cabin on her property. Customers could visit by appointment only. Clara's own house was filled with pottery of all shapes and sizes and she was well known as a pottery expert. Molly repeatedly teased her that she bought more to keep than to sell.

"You have to go to kiln openings to get the pottery at reasonable prices. Dealers can turn right around and double their money by selling the pieces they get at openings on the Internet the same day. Plus, some of these potters only make two batches a year. That puts a big limit on supply. You've got to grab them fresh out of the kiln," Clara lectured animatedly.

Molly threw her mother a sideways glance. "Sounds like a scam to me. Dealers wait for those two kiln openings a year and go crazy, buying up everything the potter has, right? I mean, the potters limit the supply and the demand increases, causing normal people to get up with the chickens. Pretty clever."

"It takes a lot of work to make this kind of pottery. We're not talking about some pansy pot or a coffee mug. These art potters may have spent ten years learning how to make something perfect come off the wheel. I can't explain it to you. You just have to see it for yourself. You'll learn to love it all—the kiln openings, the pottery festivals, outbidding someone for a piece you just have to have at auction. Trust me, it's a complete addiction! People will *absolutely* kill for this stuff, you'll see."

It took about an hour and a half to reach Seagrove from Hillsborough, and the two women pulled onto a dirt and gravel road marked with a plywood sign that read C. C. Burle Pottery in rough, worn letters. The narrow, tree-lined drive was already lined with cars as the sun began to warn the sky of its imminent arrival.

"Look at all these cars!" Molly exclaimed. She had expected to see a dozen at most.

"We're late," her mother scowled. "We are going to have a horrible place in line. Just park anywhere. Hurry, hurry!"

Molly squeezed her mother's sedan in between a makeshift row of pickup trucks and noted several other luxury cars farther up the drive toward a rusted metal barn. The mix of people gathered in front of the barn was just as interesting. There were men in overalls and others in button-downs and khaki pants. Several women wore frumpy, flowered dresses, and others dressed in pants, sweater sets, and pearls. Molly felt comfortable in her white blouse and khaki pants—one of the standard uniforms worn to a casual southern event. Her eyes, which had felt puffy and swollen in the car, now darted around wildly as she tried to soak in all the details.

"I'm going to look over the pottery. Get in line," her mother hissed urgently and prodded her forward. Molly walked quickly up the drive to a patch of scraggly grass located between the barn and the potter's workshop.

Molly got in line behind the small cluster of buyers who appeared to be calmly chatting next to a rope. The thin strip of twine served as the divider between the customers and the three tables loaded with pottery. Molly noticed that the calmness on people's faces was really a charade. Nervous glances were thrown back and forth between one's neighbor, the tables of pottery, and the ticking face of a watch. Tension sat in the air like a low, heavy thunderhead.

"This isn't too bad." Her mother returned from examining the pottery. She counted the twelve backs of the buyers ahead of her and smiled. She was pleased with their spot in line. "With two of us, we should easily get three or four pieces. Let's decide on what we're going for."

Molly followed her mother's eyes toward the pottery. In the young light, it was effused with a glow that only pieces made by hand seem to carry. Molly noticed a brown and white pitcher with a snake curling around the top. The snake's mouth was open as if to strike, revealing a red tongue and two rows of sharp, white clay teeth. As she scanned the rows of face jugs, churns, pitchers, roosters, and crocks on the other tables, more people began lining up behind them and whispering to one another.

"I like that snake pitcher," Molly announced to her mother in a normal voice.

"Shhhhh!" her mother whispered apprehensively. "Don't say what you're going for or you'll draw attention to it. Then everyone will think you've noticed something special."

"Oh, sorry," she said quietly. "Which pieces *are* we going for?"

"Those two roosters on the table to the far right, that face jug with the crying eyes on the center table, and your snake pitcher."

Molly scanned over the tables until she had located the two large red roosters with sharp, angular beaks and tails. On the center table, a jug decorated with a grotesque face leaked white glaze from its porcelain eyes. Molly grimaced.

"That's not very pretty."

"You'd change your mind if you sold it for $500 on eBay."

"Wow." Molly nodded. "So, how does this work?"

"At exactly eight o'clock, C. C. will cut the rope and everyone will make a mad dash for the pottery. You have to have a good jump off the line—that's very important."

Molly giggled. She began imagining a wild animal stampede, complete with pushing and shoving, pottery smashing, and women screaming.

"This is pretty nutty," Molly said.

"Uh huh. Just you wait," Clara said, then turned her head in the direction of a loud sound approaching the spot where they stood.

A large, black Mercedes was lumbering up the line of waiting buyers, forcing people to grudgingly step aside. The shiny car pulled right up in front of the barn, spraying dust and bits of gravel into the air. A portly man with a shock of white hair slowly lifted himself out of the driver's seat and raised his hands to the watching crowd like a conductor ready to begin a symphony.

"All right, y'all can start. The Pottery Man's here now!" he called in a loud, brassy drawl.

"Who is *that*?" Molly asked her mother, who was now frowning.

"*That* is George-Bradley Staunton. He's a big-time collector and a full-time jackass."

"Oh," said a surprised Molly, for her mother rarely used expletives.

The jackass in question began moving up the line, shaking hands with reluctant men and flirting with all the women. A partially smoked cigarette dangled from his mouth and he paused to light another one whenever he began a new conversation. He wore a white linen suit with a peach shirt and tan leather loafers. He had loose cheeks and his neck was so thick that it seemed to have swallowed his chin. The formless neck and bulging green eyes gave him the overall look of a bullfrog. He dabbed at the beads of sweat on his forehead with a ratty, monogrammed handkerchief and moved toward Molly and Clara like a king receiving the acquiescence of his subjects.

"Well now, if it isn't the beautiful Clara Appleby! And this fine lookin' lady must be your sister." Cigarette smoke was exhaled in their direction.

Molly made a visible effort not to recoil from the man's heavy hand resting on her upper arm. He leered at her and her mother, raking both of them from head to toe with his eyes while his thin lips stretched into a snakelike smile eerily like the one on the pottery pitcher.

"You two charming ladies must have gotten up purty early to come on over here and save my spot in line!" he announced, laughing. His breath smelled so strongly of tobacco that Molly almost gagged. She turned her face away and pulled in fresh air.

"Oh G. B., we're way too far back for you," her mother purred with false sweetness. "You need to be much farther up to get the good stuff."

"Young missy," he said as he stuck out his thick, clammy hand toward Molly, "I am George-Bradley Sherman Staunton IV, but you can just call me George-Bradley. Are you a new collector I now have to contend with?"

"No." She withdrew her hand quickly and wiped it on the back of her pants. "I'm a writer for *Collector's Weekly*. I'm doing a series on North Carolina potters. This is my first kiln opening."

"Well, they're all as different as marbles in a bag. I hope you've got your racin' shoes on, girl, 'cause this here big boy is after some five pieces this mornin'."

"Good luck then," Clara said and turned away in polite dismissal.

With one last lecherous glance, George-Bradley Staunton moved up the line.

"God, what a slime! Is he a used car salesman or something like that?" Molly asked.

Her mother laughed. "He doesn't really need to work.

His wife came with a very large trust fund, but officially, he's a real estate attorney. He's got 'Esquire' on his cards along with that mouthful of a name."

"He oughta have 'Sewer Breath, Esquire' on them instead."

"Oh, he's a sleaze, there's no doubt about it, but he's got the premier pottery collection of central North Carolina, next to that man at the front of the line." Clara jerked a thumb toward a nervous-looking, middle-aged man wearing a red and white checked shirt tucked into jeans.

"Who is he?" Molly asked.

"He has an odd name. Hillary Keane. He's the first one in line at any major kiln opening."

Molly observed Keane as he struggled to take off his silver spectacles. His hands looked swollen and gnarled, as if crooked branches had replaced the fingers and the knuckles had been transformed into wrinkled walnuts. Awkwardly, Keane removed his glasses and tried to clean them against his shirt, but dropped them helplessly on the ground instead. The woman next to him retrieved them, and he gave her an embarrassed smile. Fumbling, Keane replaced the glasses on his narrow nose and cast a cautious glance to the left and right before letting his anxious eyes rest feverishly on the pottery.

"Anyway," Clara returned to the original subject of their conversation, "as difficult as it may be, everyone wants to be George-Bradley's friend for those rare days when he feels like selling a piece or two."

"Have you seen his stuff?"

"Not in person. I've only heard about it from friends. His wife is always at home, and she doesn't like pottery or the people in the business, so not many are welcome there.

I'd give anything to snoop around that house. Did I ever tell you what happened at this opening last year?"

"No."

"Oh my God, this story is a legend!" She lowered her voice. "Everyone was waiting for C. C. to cut the rope, just like this. When he did, George-Bradley sprinted off to get some piece that he had to have. He knocked two people over getting to it."

Molly looked around at the tight spaces around the tables and at the size of the growing crowd. She thought about George-Bradley's wide girth. "I can see how that would happen."

"Yes, but one of the people he knocked over was an elderly lady, and she was hurt badly," Clara said seriously.

"How?"

"She broke her leg! George-Bradley shoved her so hard that she fell sideways in a twisted heap. She spent a week recovering in the hospital and had to hire someone to help her around the house. She told everyone who caused her accident too. He denied it. Never even apologized. And we all saw it with our own eyes."

"That is shameless!" Molly let a judgmental scowl fall on George-Bradley's barrel-round back.

"Oh, here come C. C. and Eileen."

The potter, wearing the traditional denim overalls that seemed to separate the potters from the collectors, moved shyly toward the line and greeted a few friends. He was in his late seventies and moved with the slow stiffness of a man who has spent dozens of years working in mills and bent over a potter's wheel. Molly noticed that the other potters were hanging off to the side, out of line, drinking coffee and humorously watching the tense buyers. One of them looked familiar.

"Isn't that Sam Chance?" she asked Clara as her eyes met those of a short, kind-faced potter with white hair and winking blue eyes. "It is!" Molly waved, and Sam held up his coffee cup in a smiling salute.

Occasionally, Sam Chance would go to area schools as a visiting artist in order to demonstrate pottery-making techniques. Last year, he had come to Molly's school, and she had watched, spellbound, as he threw jug after jug for her sixth-grade students. The art teacher had arranged for several North Carolina artists to be guest teachers for a day. Aside from Sam, there had been a folk art carver who cut up logs using a chain saw and turned them into alligators and giraffes. There had also been a storyteller who recounted Appalachian tales while having the class sketch the "feelings" her stories invoked. Molly had asked to sit in on each of these lectures and found them as rewarding as her students.

"Do all the area potters visit each other's kiln openings?" she asked her mother.

"No, only if they're friends or former apprentices. Most of these guys have learned all they know from C. C., so they come to show their support and to help wrap up the pieces after the sale."

Molly was surprised. "Wow. C. C. is older than I thought. For some reason, I pictured all of these guys as middle-aged or younger."

"Oh, C. C. is one of the last *real* traditional potters. He digs his own clay, makes his own glazes, and fires everything in a kiln he built himself. In fact, except for the ancient mule that he replaced with a tractor motor, he does everything just as the potters did it in the early 1900s."

George-Bradley's bright white suit caught Molly's eye again. Done flirting with the attractive women in the back of the line, he moved toward the potters and began shaking their hands and slapping them on the backs with overblown gusto. When he reached Sam, Molly heard him say, "Sam Chance? What are *you* doing here?" He raised his voice like a bully on the playground, hoping to seek the attention of the other children. "Don't you have some *dinner plates* to make?" He laughed as the other potters eyed him angrily. "This here is art pottery, boy. The stuff that collectors are made of."

Molly was shocked. George-Bradley had called a man at least fifteen years his senior "boy." Sam's face was blocked by George-Bradley's expansive back, where sweat was beginning to spread through the thin jacket, so Molly didn't see his reaction. Several of the other potters simply walked away, but George-Bradley rapidly cornered another, younger potter and began criticizing him on the weak color of his red glazes.

Eileen Burle, a kind-faced woman in her seventies, saved the young man from further torment by asking for his assistance. She sent him off to the house and continued walking among the crowd handing out what looked like cookies from a wooden tray. Another, younger woman in her late thirties poured out cups of coffee or cold tea. Molly noticed that she was pregnant, but her freckled face lacked any trace of an expectant glow and her eyes stared fixedly at someone in line. Her gaze was so intent that she poured a glass of tea until it overflowed the cup. Blinking, she nervously cleaned up the mess and loaded up a tray in order to serve the waiting throng, which had now grown to almost two hundred people.

From her place toward the front of the line, Molly couldn't believe how many people had congregated behind her. There were at least one hundred eager buyers wringing their hands and talking loudly with bursts of nervous excitement as the rope-cutting moment drew near.

Her mother introduced her to C. C. as he made his way to where they stood.

"This your first openin'? You're in for a treat. My wife told me to go by the lottery system, where folks pick a number out of a hat, but this is too much fun to give up." He smiled, snipping his scissors in the air.

"Can you tell me something about that kiln, Mr. Burle?" Molly gestured toward the dome of bricks and wood sticking out of the ground a few hundred yards behind the pottery tables. It resembled an overturned ship whose rounded hull closely hugged the earth. At one end was an arched opening in the bricks that looked like a miniature railroad tunnel entrance.

"Call me C. C. Now, that kiln is called a groundhog kiln, 'cause it sits kind of squat against the ground. I've got to crawl on in there to load the pottery, then stoke it with wood, then heat it up good and hot for a few days. In the last couple of hours, we feed that fire like crazy and smoke comes pouring out the chimney there." He pointed toward the end of the kiln. "That's called the 'blast off' time. That's when you can look in at yer pots and they's as red as the devil, just a-lookin' at ya through all that heat."

Molly watched the pride flush his face as he looked over at his finished pots. He pointed at a gallon jug with a greenish, earth-tone glaze.

"That glaze is called 'Seagrove slip' and it's been made in these parts for more than a hundred years. My Daddy made it that way and his Daddy and his Daddy did too. It's our family recipe."

"I'd love to ask you more questions after the sale, if

that's OK." Molly told him about the pottery articles she planned to write.

"Sure, I'll take you around and show you all the tricks. You got yer eye on somethin' out there?" He looked in the direction of the waiting pottery.

Molly nodded as he winked. "Good," he said merrily. "'Cause it's time to fetch it then."

C. C. moved over to the thin piece of rope, scissors in hand. The noise in the yard ceased like a stone falling off the edge of a cliff. Just then, George-Bradley brazenly shoved his bulk between the potter and the first person in line, the nervous man named Hillary Keane. The man stared at George-Bradley, his mouth opening and closing like a landed fish gasping for air. George-Bradley completely ignored Keane's look of silent outrage.

Smiling wickedly, George-Bradley leaned over to Keane and elbowed him roughly in the side. "My dear little man, what are *you* doing here? You know all the pieces you want could possibly be snagged and bought by yours truly. Ha! Why don't you just give up now and try to save face? I am the King of Kiln Openings!" Then, as if emphasizing Keane's hopelessness, George-Bradley dropped his empty Styrofoam cup onto the ground in front of Keane's feet and crushed it with an Italian leather loafer.

Rage drained Keane's face of all color. "Bastard!" he yelled, inhaling a great swallow of breath in order to release a stream of hatred at the rude collector beside him, but at that moment, C. C. severed the rope.

"Wait for me!" George-Bradley tried to bellow in protest, but his mouth was too crammed full of cookies to be heard clearly.

The crowd lurched forward as one body, shoving one another out of the way as each person moved toward a table. Molly headed for the nearest piece, the face jug with the greenish glaze and the white, crying eyes. As she reached out to grasp it, a thick, sweaty arm pushed her away so roughly that she lost her balance and fell to the ground. With a smarting elbow and stains on her shirt and pants, Molly stood up again quickly and looked around to see George-Bradley shrug his wide shoulders in mock apology.

"Bastard," Molly muttered as she watched him disappear into the writhing crowd. She gritted her teeth and shoved herself forward, knocking into another man who was reaching toward the same piece. She grabbed the green face jug and began to fight her way toward the table where the snake pitcher was.

Chaos reigned. Bodies collided and bounced off one another in every direction. Arms and hands reached out everywhere, and angry curses were issued in sharp staccato among shouts of delight and disappointment. These noises were punctuated by gasps of pain as feet were stepped on, ribs were jabbed, or two pieces of pottery bumped one another too hard, chipping the glaze or breaking a jug handle.

Molly darted through a small opening in the squirming throng, and though she was neither quick nor agile, she was determined to get her piece. She saw with relief that it was still on the table. Pottery was being grabbed like it was on fire, and as she made her move to grasp the handle of the snake pitcher, she saw George-Bradley out of the corner of her eye, wrestling a large jug with the face of a devil out of a petite woman's arms.

"I had it first!" she protested, but he was too strong for her, and she released the piece and moved on to find another, her face a mask of anger.

The victorious scoundrel examined his piece for a millisecond with a look of pure greed and satisfaction, then returned to the fray. Disgusted, Molly looked for her mother, spotting her as she seized the second red rooster from the back table. Their eyes met for a second, and they lifted their pieces in the air to show each other their successes before the crowd blocked their view.

As Molly turned around to make her way back to the safety of the lawn, she saw George-Bradley's face beyond a threesome of buyers arguing over a double-handed vase. Eyes darting about frantically, he searched for another treasure. Suddenly, he raised his head and howled in pain, his eyes bulging even farther from their sockets. In another flash, Molly's view was blocked, and then she saw George-Bradley stagger off toward the side of the barn, out of sight.

Curious, Molly held her pottery against her ample chest and followed. She poked her head around the corner of the sheet metal wall and stopped in her tracks. George-Bradley stood leaning against the side of the barn, his devil jug and another crying face jug resting on the ground at his feet. As she watched, George-Bradley examined a tiny, red stain on his peach shirt. Undoing the last two buttons, he exposed a roll of pasty flesh and rubbed at his flaccid skin with moistened fingertips. He repeated this motion several times, more and more slowly each time. His downcast mouth frowned in confusion. And then, his eyes lifted and stared off beyond Molly, registering a look of surprised realization.

Abruptly, someone propelled Molly away from the corner of the barn and into the clearing. It was Clara.

"You've got to protect your pieces once you've got them, honey," Clara said, unaware of George-Bradley's odd posture. The two red roosters were already tucked neatly into one of the plastic bins, which Clara had strategically hidden behind the trunk of a pine tree.

The tight knots of struggling people had dispersed and only a few buyers remained around the tables, still playing a verbal tug-of-war over a vase or jug.

"That was crazy!" Molly said breathlessly as she looked around. Her bizarre image of George-Bradley was replaced by the memory of grabbing her fabulous snake pitcher.

"Wonderful, isn't it?" Clara beamed.

"Actually, yes. I have to admit, that was like being on a roller coaster. Thirty seconds of pure adrenaline and it's still pumping."

Molly looked around for George-Bradley's bulky form, but he was nowhere to be found.

"Let's get in line to pay," Clara said.

As they moved into the checkout line, the tension that had permeated the air all morning had vanished, replaced by a vibrant camaraderie, which induced a great deal of backslapping and cheek kissing among the fellow collectors. Buyers congratulated one another as if they had just returned from a dangerous mission in space, holding out their new pieces, admiring how each was made or glancing sorrowfully as a desired piece went home with another owner.

Molly felt pretty smug and friendly herself, chatting with those in front of her in line and complimenting a woman next to her on her beautiful brown and beige swirl tea pitcher. She held out her snake pitcher for praise as if it were a newborn child instead of her first piece of pottery.

Molly turned back to her mother's gleaming face. "It's just like a good auction," Clara said. "You're all enemies while it's going on, but in the end, you're all friends again. It's pretty much the same group of people at all of these openings, so you may as well call a truce at the end of the day."

"And no one even looks at the prices." Molly noticed the tag tied to her piece. "Are you all this insane?"

"Yes. It makes us a tight group." Clara's eyes narrowed as she noticed a green and brown stain on her daughter's pants. "What happened to your clothes? You've got grass stains."

Molly was just opening her mouth to tell her mother about the appalling behavior of George-Bradley when a cry of "Help!" from behind one of the pottery tables rose above the noise.

Molly craned her head to see that the man whose name was on the tip of her tongue was lying facedown in the grass, almost hidden by the other tables. He was completely still, his face an immoveable white mask. Next to his outstretched hand lay the devil face jug, the one he had snatched away just moments before from the petite woman.

Clara drew in a sharp breath, taking in the shocking scene. She grabbed Molly's arm, then just as suddenly relaxed her grip.

"Thank God!" Clara exhaled the words, her eyes glued on the pottery jug where it rested in the grass. "It didn't break."

Chapter 2

Perhaps an ideal future lies ahead when the world will be divided not by ideologies, but into those who make pots and those who buy them.

—ROSEMARY ZORZA, FROM *POTTERY: CREATING WITH CLAY*

For a moment, no one moved. Then a man bent over George-Bradley and checked for a pulse.

"It's weak," he said to no one in particular. "Someone better call 9-1-1."

From where she stood, Molly watched the man unbutton George-Bradley's sweat-stained shirt. He asked others to lend a hand moving his heavy burden into the shade until help arrived. Two of the potters attempted to pick George-Bradley up, but reconsidered. Instead, they carried over a large plywood board, which they balanced on the seats of three chairs. Their lean-to prevented the sun from shining directly onto the immobile form, but only made the paleness of his face seem more noticeable. Ten minutes ago George-Bradley had been flushed with excitement, but now his pallid and expressionless face sagged like limp dough.

The crowd was silent. Once the potters had sprung into

action, a few people began whispering in hushed tones. Ice broken, the entire crowd began muttering to one another in a tone of nervous excitement.

Nearby, a woman started crying. Molly noted that it was the same petite woman who had been holding the devil jug before George-Bradley wrenched it away. Molly turned to her mother and quietly told her about the incident.

"Her?" Her mother pointed to the weeping figure without bothering to be quiet at all. "That bag of bones is a total actress. Don't go feeling too sorry for her. She and George-Bradley have shared a *past,* and now that it's over they fight like cats and dogs at these sales. They also try to outbid each other at every auction just to get the other's goat. She's just searching for attention." They watched as two men offered her tissues. Clara snorted. "Looks like she got it, too."

Molly examined the other woman enviously. Short and thin, she looked elegant in a beige, short-sleeved sweater, cream-colored skirt, and gold jewelry. Her blonde hair was swept up in a glossy twist and her shoes weren't even dusty. Molly, who was a full-figured size fourteen, always wondered how it would feel to be as tiny and trim as this woman.

"She's wearing panty hose!" her mother exclaimed in disgust, looking at her daughter's expression. Clara knew how Molly felt about herself. "In *this* heat."

That was a formal dismissal. Wearing panty hose anywhere was an uncomfortable burden that the Appleby women avoided at all costs. Wearing them to a kiln opening was unbelievable.

Before they could continue berating the theatrically weeping woman, one of the potters sitting next to George-Bradley gestured urgently to one of his friends. The second man quickly knelt and felt for a pulse on George-Bradley's neck. His eyes instantly grew round in panic and after a moment's hesitation, in which he glanced helplessly at the potter beside him, he began to perform CPR.

As Molly watched the two men attempt to revive George-Bradley's lifeless figure, the paramedics arrived. The crowd parted as the ambulance backed up in a series of loud bleeps, directed by one of the potters. Three paramedics hustled over to the prone figure with kits and a gurney. Bending over George-Bradley, they worked hurriedly, their faces set and completely unreadable. Within minutes, he was lifted into the ambulance. One paramedic continued performing CPR inside while a second briefly questioned the potter who had checked for George-Bradley's pulse. As the paramedic hopped back into the ambulance, Molly could see him look at his patient and shake his head. Then the doors were closed and the ambulance pulled away, its sirens eerily silent.

The crowd watched the vehicle progress down the drive. Despite the event, not many people had moved from their spots. Unsure of how to act, they simply waited to see what would happen next. Once the source of their shock was removed, they just continued checking out as if nothing unusual had happened.

"Do you think he's all right?" some people asked without much genuine concern. George-Bradley may have been respected in person, but behind his back, tongues wagged.

"Didn't look too good to me. I heard he has some kind of serious diabetes."

"Really? Well, did you see him goin' at those cookies? I thought you couldn't eat like that if you had his condition."

"His condition is called 'Too Many Big Macs,' if you ask me," a woman laughed.

"I'd call it too much smoking and beer chugging," added another.

One of the local dealers, a handsome man in his midforties wearing a denim shirt tucked into dark brown pants approached a cluster of buyers waiting in line to pay.

"Oh, *I* know what his condition is," he said importantly.

"Well?" a woman holding a large vase with speckled glaze demanded. "What would that be?"

"When an ambulance leaves without using its sirens," he explained, "it can only mean one thing."

The buyers looked back and forth at one another, realization slowly dawning in their eyes.

"What you saw leaving here, my friends," the man in the blue shirt declared, "was a corpse."

The excitement of George-Bradley's fatal emergency had renewed the energy of the crowd. Gossiping at a mile a minute, men and women alike paid for their items and got in their cars, eager to be the first to spread the tale of his death around town.

Molly was shocked at their flippant reactions. She had just seen her first dead body, and she felt as though her mind wasn't working correctly. She couldn't seem to move her legs and as the line moved forward, she simply stood still as other buyers went around her, paid, and left.

Finally, it was only Clara and Molly left in the quiet yard. Clara comforted Eileen, who suddenly looked years older with the excitement of the kiln opening and the shock of having one of the area's most notorious collectors collapse in her yard. Clara and the older woman began clearing up the refreshments as they murmured together in low tones.

Molly felt that this was certainly not the time to interview C. C., but he caught her eye and waved her over to
the barn.

"I can come back at a better time," she offered.

"Nah." He shook his head. "I need somethin' else to
think about instead of folks dyin' at my openin'. Come on,
I'll show you around." C. C. seemed instantly relieved at
having another subject to focus on. Molly got the whole
tour of the pottery studio, which was housed inside the
barn, the kiln, and a few treasured pieces kept inside the
small house that were crafted by generations of Burles
long gone.

C. C. showed Molly how he worked throughout the year
in the small barn that looked like a miniature metal cabin.
He had a fan for the summer and a space heater for the
winter as his only comforts. The flooring was mud-covered
concrete, cool even in the summer. The entire length of the
back wall was lined with tall wooden shelves used as drying racks. The rest of the room's accoutrements looked
reminiscent of colonial times. A crude three-legged stool
was pulled up to a wheel that used foot power instead of
electricity. An old door on sawhorses served as a table for
holding blocks of clay wrapped in tight plastic to retain
moisture. Wooden tools resembling spatulas or cheese
knives were stuck haphazardly in chipped crocks near the
wheel. Lined up on a warped tabletop were a dozen undec-
orated jugs that still looked moist to the touch. Every tool
and piece of furniture was encrusted with clay.

"I just threw them this mornin'." C. C. pointed at the
jugs with a gnarled and chapped finger. "Couldn't sleep.
Those new jugs that haven't been burned yet are called
'greenware.' See, I've turned them on the wheel but they
haven't been in the kiln yet. They'll dry out for a bit and

then go in the fire for a good, long roastin'. Come on in the house and I'll show you some old pieces."

Molly trailed after the spry, older man on a gravel path that wandered behind the barn. Tucked neatly into the woods, their unpainted house looked as though it had always belonged in the copse of trees.

Inside, Molly noticed that the Burles lived a simple life. Their sparse furniture was easily twenty years old and the rusty hue of the shaggy carpet hinted that it too had been around for some time. Pulling pots off of a nearby bookshelf, C. C. showed her one piece with grapes on it that his grandmother had made out of rolled balls of clay and applied one by one to the jug that his grandfather had turned hours earlier. Afterwards, she had incised some leaves and curled vines to create a beautiful and delicate design.

Molly handled the piece gently, admiring the form, the lightness, and the grace of the grapevine.

"Can it hold water?" she asked.

"Tight as Noah's Ark," C. C. answered. "After all, the Burles made this stuff for people around here to actually use. Local people made butter and cream in our churns and stored all kinds of foodstuffs in these crocks. This buying pottery just to look at is all pretty new around here."

"What's the history of this piece?" Molly asked, holding up a piece that looked like two jugs stacked on top of each other with spouts sticking out in opposite directions.

"That there is a monkey jug. See, you put liquor in its bottom half and a water chaser in the top. These are actually two jugs fired on top of one another so they have separate compartments. Now, you get yerself a nice cup, pour some whiskey from this bottom section"—C. C. tapped the spout of the bigger half of the jug—"then turn it around"— he swiveled the jug so that the opposite spout on the top half faced forward—"then add yer water. You've got a cocktail party all in one place. Me, I like how the whiskey half is so much bigger than the water half."

Molly laughed as she admired the jug's speckled glaze. It looked exactly like the glaze on the pieces C. C. had put out for sale this morning.

"Could you tell me more about the family recipe?" she asked, pointing at the glaze.

"Now, that's fun. You get out your mixer and add one part powdered glass (we have a machine to break it up), one part ash from burned wood, and one part slip."

"Slip?"

"Slip is some broken greenware mixed with water."

"So you blend all that stuff and get some greenish icing for your cake."

"That's right, and we keep it all in a big barrel and dip a piece right into it. Gotta make sure there's none on the bottom or that piece will stick like glue to the kiln floor when it gets fired."

Molly examined a few more pieces on his shelf. She could see that even though the recipe for glaze was the same, each piece had a unique pattern of flecks, blotches, and drips. She picked up a beautiful crock that had a swirl decoration in green and beige.

"How do you make the glaze into that swirl pattern?"

"That's not the glaze," said C. C. smiling. "That's two different colors of clay. The secret to makin' swirl is somethin' I only share with other potters. You get yourself a wheel and I'll teach you."

"I think that would be wonderful," Molly said, and she meant it, but her few attempts to make pottery were disasters. Her finished products were wobbly, without symmetry, and plain unattractive.

When the tour concluded, Molly's head was stuffed with new details about the Burle family and their pottery. She was touched by how C. C. handled each piece with an intimate tenderness, by the pride he took in carrying on his family trade, and his excitement in teaching a new generation of potters the traditional methods handed down by men like himself for so many years.

He had been creating useable art since the 1930s. His hands were arthritic, but they still turned perfect vessels and guided the hands of future artisans. Words were whirling around Molly's head, impatient to do justice to this gifted man. She couldn't wait to write her article.

After thanking C. C. and Eileen for their time and offering awkward condolences for the negative ending of the opening, Molly met her mother at the car. As they kicked up dust going down the driveway, Molly looked back wistfully in the rearview mirror at the empty tables that were once laden with pottery. Her thoughts turned back to the large mass of George-Bradley's body being loaded into the ambulance. The morning had been more eventful than she could have ever imagined.

"Where to?" Molly asked her mother, as she examined the brownish flecks freckling the green glaze of her snake pitcher, trying to put all thoughts of dead bodies out of her mind.

"Let's go to lunch. All this drama makes me hungry."

Chapter 3

About all the potters that I knew lived to be up in their eighties, so I don't see where pottin' had killed any of them. Something's gonna take you away from here sometime or another anyway!

—BURLON CRAIG, CATAWBA VALLEY POTTER, FROM *FOXFIRE 8*

The Jugtown Café didn't look like much on the outside, but the locals and pottery hounds all knew that it was the place to eat when visiting Seagrove. Though it was between the times of breakfast and lunch for most, the lot was filled with cars and trucks.

Inside, pottery displays on high shelves lined the perimeter of the room. Molly and Clara were seated below a row of menacing face jugs with large mouths and chipped teeth. They got the last table by the front door, relieved to be in the path of outside air since the air-conditioning was set to sub zero.

"It's freezing in here!" Molly rubbed her bare arms.

"Coffee?" her mother begged a passing waitress who carried a stack of empty plates covered with brown gravy.

At the next table, four men were finishing breakfasts of ham, eggs scrambled with cheese, bacon, toast, and biscuits with gravy. One of them caught Molly staring and smiled.

"We had to roll hay today," he offered. "Makes a man mighty hungry."

"I must have gotten up this morning at your regular time," she said, saluting him with her coffee mug. "Don't know how you guys do it."

"It's been a hard summer with this drought." He shook his head, and lines of worry sprouted around his eyes and the corners of his mouth.

Molly searched for something to say, but couldn't think of anything. The lack of rain since last winter had put the Carolinas in the worst drought witnessed for over sixty years. Many farmers had lost all of their crops or had to put down their cattle because they couldn't keep them fed and watered. The clover and alfalfa crops had turned into fields of brown bramble. With the exception of the few well-irrigated farms, the summer crops were goners. Large amounts of hay were only available from the Midwest, and at high prices, so the Carolina farmers who couldn't afford it were selling or slaughtering their entire herds months earlier than usual. No one could remember a time when meat and produce prices were higher, and it irritated the Carolinians to have to buy their food from the unwholesome state of California.

Life was so different out here from Molly's little subdivision in Durham. Only two hours away, her neighborhood was filled with two-car families who worked and went to school in air-conditioned rooms. They rode bikes and went to the mall, rented movies, and ate out twice a week. Here, men struggled with the earth. They planted seed or pulled forth clay. Their backs were bent and their hands were weary. Their faces were crisscrossed with lines and turned into tanned leather by the sun.

She looked around at some other men in the room. Undoubtedly they worked in the local furniture mill eight hours each day, their lungs breathing in thin air beneath the false glow of fluorescent lights. Their hands too, she saw, seemed to belong to those of much older men.

Returning her gaze to her own table Molly examined her mother as she studied her menu. Tall and thin with dark hair, Clara had a regal presence that came from a mixture of intelligence, confidence, and good looks. She scowled and narrowed her gray eyes as she searched for their waitress, motioning across the room toward her empty coffee cup. Molly smiled at her impatience, her own gray eyes twinkling with amusement. She felt revived by the strong, sweet coffee.

"Tell me more about George-Bradley," Molly prompted after they had given their breakfast orders to the harried waitress. "You said he had a juicy past."

"Well, it's not an unusual story. Often, a collecting person will marry someone who has no interest in what they collect. You can try to get them interested by bringing them to sales or to auctions or by telling them about the incredible workmanship of an item, but you can't *make* someone be passionate about it. I think people are born as collectors, or they're not. You have to have The Gene. George-Bradley's wife, Bunny, didn't have it."

"The Gene?"

"Yes. You see, he'd go to sales and shows and she would stay home or go shopping. She never went with him on the road, and she hated every piece he brought into the house. I've heard this right from the horse's mouth. It got so they practically divided the house in half so that all of his 'ugly things' were in his half."

"Well, some of those face jugs can be pretty scary. Not the type of thing to put in your guest room."

"True, but what happened was that George-Bradley spent more and more time with people who shared his passion, especially women. That woman you saw this morning, I think her name is Susan something, she wouldn't normally be attracted to someone with George-Bradley's looks, but when you find someone who loves what you love, it can change the way you look at them."

"So why doesn't he just get divorced?"

"Who knows? Bunny knows about his running around, but she doesn't ask for a divorce either. Marriages are funny. You never know what's really going on behind closed doors."

The waitress arrived with delicious crepe-style pancakes, eggs, and burnt bacon, as requested. Molly poured some pecan syrup in a thin drizzle over the melting pat of butter in the center of her light and savory pancakes.

Her mother raised her eyebrows as she watched Molly pour, but seemed to change her mind about saying anything about her eating habits. Her daughter was on the plump side with her round hips and ample bosom, but she was also a lovely woman. Clara always marveled at her daughter's flawless and luminescent skin and the sweep of long, dark eyelashes framing eyes that always held a glint of amusement.

Such beauty and intelligence should not go to waste, Clara thought. "Now, speaking of marriage—" she began.

"Don't start," Molly interrupted. "I just haven't found the right guy."

"But you're thirty now. You'd better get going. I want grandchildren before you put me in the nursing home."

Molly sighed. "I'm working on it, and if you keep nagging me, you're going to that home a lot earlier than you'd like."

As her mother fantasized aloud about where to hold the wedding reception, Molly's thoughts wandered to Mark Harrison, the marketing director of her newspaper. She had had a crush on him the moment she joined the staff, but even after two years, they had barely exchanged more than a quick greeting in the break room or a wave while passing in the hall. Molly could see into Mark's office from her desk, and for two years she had furtively studied his tall frame and watched his shy smile as he talked on the phone or worked on his computer.

As she wondered for the millionth time whether Mark had a girlfriend, her mother plowed full steam ahead on her usual litany regarding the family engagement ring that awaited Molly in Clara's jewelry box. Molly was finally saved by a group of newcomers who seated themselves in the neighboring booth. All three women were talking at the same time like a gaggle of geese so that it was difficult to distinguish what was being said.

As they settled themselves into their seats however, it was clear that one woman was in the middle of speaking about George-Bradley. Molly and Clara's ears perked up.

"This morning, at C. C. Burle's opening," the woman continued, relating her story to her two wide-eyed friends.

"What happened?"

"Well, Trish said he just keeled on over. Boom. Landed right on the grass without hurtin' a hair on a single piece of pottery."

"Did he have a heart attack?" her friend asked.

"I don't know. Trish said they picked him up in an ambulance and took him away. He was white as a sheet in bleach, but that's all I know. He was stuffing cookies in his mouth like they were goin' out of style, that's for sure. With the shape he's in, it could have been anything."

"Did he cut in line at this one too, I wonder?"

"Of course he did! Right in front of Hillary Keane. *And* Trish said he grabbed a face jug right out of Susan Black's hands. She was spittin' mad."

"I don't know who he thinks he is, that George-Bradley," one of the women snarled. "When I was first collecting, he took an old crock right out of my hands at a tag sale. He told me it was damaged and I wouldn't want it. Stuck it in front of my face and said, 'See? Look at all them scratches.' Then he put a different crock in my hands and said, 'Allow me to advise you. Buy this one.' And stupid me, I bought it. I found out later that the *scratched* crock actually had a poem written on it about the potter's wife. It was late nineteenth century and worth over $1,000. I hate that man!"

Her friends murmured in agreement.

"Still, I don't wish a heart attack on anyone." The woman sighed reluctantly as if that's exactly what she wished. "If that's what happened."

"Oh, we're going to find out," announced the third woman triumphantly, holding up a cell phone. "You know Randy, that guy I dated for a while over at Asheboro General? I asked him to page me with a text message once he finds out what's goin' on with George-Bradley."

Molly and Clara exchanged looks. They were done with their meals and their plates had been cleared. Normally, they would be getting up to leave, but suddenly the morning's events, combined with a full stomach, rendered them immobile. They lingered over their cups of tepid coffee and openly eavesdropped.

As the women in the next booth placed their order, one of them said, "I wish we knew exactly what happened. Call that Randy and find out."

"I already tried. I'm sure George-Bradley will end up being fine. He'll be back at the next kiln opening breaking the bones of little old ladies and pushing people like me into the dirt."

Clara could contain herself no longer. She couldn't resist leaving her neighbors unenlightened.

"No, he won't," she cut into their conversation with authority. "His days of being the rudest, greediest man in Asheboro are over."

"Really?" asked one of the women.

"Yep," Clara said as she stood and placed a few dollars on the table. "He's dead."

Molly also stood, watching the women's faces digest the news. She felt suddenly uneasy. Shouldn't they all be feeling more than curiosity? Someone was dead. A man's life was over. Molly was ready to go home.

Above her head, the face jugs seemed to be smiling crooked, sinister smiles from their lofty positions above the diners, their pointed teeth and slanted eyes gleaming sharp white from within the shadows.

Chapter 4

The best pieces of pottery bring out in most of us an almost overwhelming desire to touch, caress, and hold them.

—PETER COSENTINO, *THE ENCYCLOPEDIA OF POTTERY TECHNIQUES*

The trio of woman at the Jugtown Café thanked Clara and she and Molly finally headed home. The June sun was searing the ground and the humidity hung like a damp washcloth over the sky. The car was stuffy and filled with thick air. It was a typical summer day in North Carolina, the kind that drained people of energy and made them seek the shelter of rooms with air-conditioning or at least a ceiling fan.

"Let's take the back way," Clara suggested as she discovered her driving glasses in the side pocket of her purse. Replete with her tasty lunch, Molly eased the passenger seat back and stretched out her long legs.

Avoiding the interstates, the "back way" took them through flat farmland and quirky crossroads following a crooked trail from Seagrove to Pittsboro, which was just south of Chapel Hill. Clara always returned this way if she wasn't pressed for time. She enjoyed the rural scenery and the lack of large trucks and other noisy traffic.

They passed several pottery shops on the way and Molly noted how different the signs for each pottery were. Some had been like C. C.'s sign—simple, hand-painted lettering on a white wood board. Some were even more rustic and were so faded that it was hard to distinguish the name. Others were sparkling new and were clearly made by professional sign makers. Their raised gold or green letters caught the eye and different graphic designs of purple pots or rainbow vases were a sharp contrast to the plain letters wobbling across a board.

Molly studied her brochure on Seagrove, which she had borrowed from her mother before suggesting the article to her editor. More than one hundred potteries were speckled over an area of about twenty-five miles. Though they were visited by busloads of tourists every year, it didn't seem possible that all of the potters could earn a living from their trade. After all, Molly had never even heard of the area until her mother mentioned it, and she had lived in North Carolina for ten years.

Her mother informed her that many of the potters had full-time jobs. Some worked in the local mills or canneries, some raised livestock, and others worked as guest artists at schools around the state. Most of the potters were men. If they were married, their wives watched the "shop," which was often just a painted shed, while their husbands went to work. Over the weekends, the potters would turn and burn (an expression for creating pieces using the wheel then firing them in a kiln). Children of pottery families helped with the shop and if they showed the talent for it, began turning pieces or helping apply glaze at an early age.

This family lifestyle that centered on clay had been in place for over three hundred years in rural North Carolina.

Molly learned that most of the pottery was no longer made in the traditional way, because very few potters could afford to pursue their craft on a full-time basis. Many now bought premixed clay and glazes to save time. Some potters even had commercial kilns, but most built their own, priding themselves on creating the vessel that would burn their wares. They often cut pine slabs from their own yards to feed the kiln's flames.

The potteries Clara drove by grew more spread out from one another as they left the heart of Seagrove behind them. Some, like Jugtown Pottery, were down small lanes slightly off the beaten path. The location never hindered their success. Hundreds of buyers and apprentices alike had traveled for decade after decade to seek the wares and knowledge of the family of potters who had been in that spot for generations.

Thin forests slowly gave way to pastures. Cows mingled lazily beneath the shade of ancient oak trees or slumped near the banks of small streams, searching for any available refuge from the heat. Both women were quiet in the car, conscious of the fact that they had both just seen George-Bradley alive and well a few hours ago and now, just like that, he was dead.

"I feel sorry for him," Molly said, breaking the silence.

"Why?"

"Well, it seems to me that he was, you know, kind of lonely. Yeah, he probably deserved it for being a first-class jerk to most people, but is anyone going to miss him now that he's gone?"

Her mother shook her head. "I don't think so. That rude behavior at the kiln opening was so typical of George-

Bradley. He was ungentlemanly, condescending to anyone who he thought was a class below him, even to the potters. Yet he felt that his money and his collection earned him a place of honor in everyone's eyes. Maybe he has family who will grieve, but I can't think of anyone I know who will."

"Yet everyone knows his name. All of Randolph County knew who he was and everyone in the pottery circle as well. But no one will care. See, it's kind of sad."

"They'll care about his pottery, that's for sure. All the sharks will be circling poor Bunny. People would die to get their hands on George-Bradley's collection."

"And she hated it all, right? So won't she want to sell it?"

"You never know. She might want to hang onto it for a while. She might want to give it away to a museum. She might want to throw every piece against the wall. I don't know Bunny well. Like I said, she went her way and George-Bradley went his. Where that pottery is going to end up is a riddle I would love to know the answer to."

"Listen, Ma. I feel like there's something not quite right about his death. I didn't think to tell you this before, but he was acting really weird toward the end of the . . . the grabbing session." Molly described what she had witnessed behind the barn.

"Rubbing his stomach?" Clara wondered. "I've heard of grabbing your left arm during a heart attack, but this is a new one."

"What would explain why he went behind the barn to unbutton his shirt? And why was he so out of it? It was like . . . I don't know, like he was drugged." The vision of George-Bradley's confused face nagged at her.

Clara pursed her lips. "Well, there certainly were plenty of people there who'd like to see him dead. Anyone who collects has to fight him off at every sale, but if it wasn't an accident, the police will find out," she added with finality.

"Maybe they will," Molly replied. Then because she didn't think her mother was taking her at all seriously, she added, "Or maybe *I* will."

Molly drove up to her little house feeling completely spent. Her cool, cozy rooms had never seemed so inviting. She sank down on her couch with a soda and some catalogues from her mail pile. Within seconds, a tan tabby hopped on her lap and began "making biscuits" with his claws on her stomach.

"Oww! Griffin! Here, have a nice pile of junk mail to sit on instead."

Molly made a pleasant nest of envelopes and realtor advertisements for her cat. He happily relocated and circled himself into bathing position.

"I swear, you are the vainest cat in all of Durham."

As Molly glanced over the glossy pages of Pottery Barn's fall collection, she felt her body slowly relaxing. Griffin's steady purring and the whir of the air conditioner soon sent her off to sleep.

The sound of the phone ringing jarred both her and the tabby into an upright position, both blinking in surprise against the afternoon light.

"Hello?" she croaked.

"Are you asleep when you should be in here typing up that article?" demanded the grating voice of her editor, Carl Swanson. He paused to take a suck on his cigarette. "I expect that piece on my desk by Monday!"

Carl was an overweight chain-smoker with a truculent nature and an obsession with the paper's circulation rate.

The staff lived in fear of his moody nature and horrible breath—a consistent blend of nicotine and coffee.

"I was at the kiln opening at dawn," Molly said defensively. "I certainly got enough information for an article, but maybe a little more excitement than I bargained for. However"—she gave a theatrical pause—"this might be just the article to help our sales. A famous collector died today, Carl. But that's not all." She paused again, wondering if she was about to say something she would later regret, but the nagging feeling that followed her home from the kiln opening would not let go. "I don't think his death was accidental."

Molly could almost see her boss sitting up straighter in his chair, the ashes from his cigarette falling onto his expansive lap.

"Well? Go on, girlie! Give me all the details and let's see what we can print!"

Molly ignored his customary display of chauvinism and gave him a blow-by-blow account of the morning's events. Swanson was completely keyed up over the idea of publishing such a dramatic story.

"Get in here right away. I want you to go over the details with Mark Harrison."

Molly's heart skipped a beat. "Why Mark?"

"He went to med school at Duke. Didn't finish, but he's got some buddies in hospitals around here and we need those medical details to be accurate. Can't have you writing the wrong stuff and getting us sued."

Molly scowled at the implication that she would mess up and hung up on her boss as he began a coughing fit. Then she immediately brightened at the thought of seeing Mark.

* * *

Twenty minutes later, she arrived at the paper's offices in northern Durham and made her way to the ladies room, where she applied some lipstick and ran a brush through her straight, dark hair.

Swanson must have briefed Mark, for he was waiting for her with his desk cleared.

"I didn't know you went to med school," she began.

A shadow crossed Mark's face. "Yeah, but I didn't finish. Listen," he said, hastening to change the subject, "why don't you tell me everything that happened this morning. Swanson has indicated that you think this collector's death might be suspicious? Is that true?"

Molly nodded, sensing a strong amount of doubt in Mark's voice. Still, she related her story once again, and he listened intently while occasionally jotting down a few notes. He was clearly more interested in George-Bradley's medical demise than in the descriptions of the pottery or the behavior of the buyers when the rope was cut.

"So you heard that he had diabetes?"

"Yes, someone in line mentioned it after he was taken away," Molly said.

Mark asked, "Did he look healthy?"

"No. He was overweight and sweating a lot. He kept dabbing at his face with a handkerchief. Plus, he was drinking tea and eating cookies like mad."

"Sweet tea?"

Molly laughed. "Boy, you give away that you're not from around here every time you ask something like that. Of course it was sweet tea! Is there any other kind?"

Mark ignored her teasing. "It sounds like he didn't treat himself too well."

"Not in *that* regard." She proceeded to fill him in on the

gossip about his affairs and his unusual marriage, pleased that she felt so comfortable talking to him. "The Stauntons," she concluded, "were a couple divided by his pottery collection. He collected it. She hated it."

"Well, I don't collect stuff, unless you count my beer bottle collection or my jar of wine corks. Does that mean I have to marry someone who likes beer bottles?"

Molly laughed. "I don't think that all married couples have that problem. After all, it's much more economical if only one person is spending money on stuff."

"Well, I'm a cheapskate bachelor, so no problem there."

A bachelor! Did he say that to let her know he was available? Molly met Mark's light blue eyes but he looked away quickly and began to shuffle a pile of paper on his desk.

"Listen," he began, still looking at his desk, "I am going to call in a favor from a friend over at Asheboro General. I'll find out the medical details. If there *is* something suspicious about this guy's death, and I'm not saying there is, medical science will bring it to light. Swanson wants this piece out on Monday, so why don't you start the article and I'll give you the filler you need by tonight. We could . . ." Molly watched as Mark stumbled for words and a ruddy blush crept up his cheeks.

"Order Chinese," she suggested quickly.

"Great." He smiled, and Molly returned to her desk and began typing up her article with a zippy rhythm.

By dinnertime, Molly was growing tired. Mark stopped by her desk as she was stifling a yawn.

"You'd better knock off for tonight," he said kindly. "We can go to that fondue restaurant next door. I'll write it off as a company expense."

"Yes, please. I can finish this up in the morning," she agreed gratefully.

After the waiter took their order for spicy cheese fondue, house salads, and an entrée of meat and seafood fondue, Mark seemed to become fidgety. He crumpled and smoothed his napkin and glanced around the room, looking everywhere but at Molly.

"So did you talk to your friend at Asheboro General?" Molly asked, hoping to make him comfortable by sticking to work topics.

"Yes. Turns out that *is* the hospital where that collector guy was taken. My friend was doing his rotation in the ER when they brought him in, DOA."

Molly looked at him blankly. What did that string of acronyms mean?

"DOA?"

Mark laughed. "Oh, sorry. It means Dead On Arrival."

"He didn't even make it to the hospital?" Molly was surprised. So the customer at C. C.'s who had said that an ambulance leaving without its sirens blaring meant their patient was already dead had been correct.

"No. And guess what he died from?"

"I don't know. Heart attack?"

"No."

Molly thought about what else might have afflicted an overweight man. "Stroke?"

"No."

"Brain aneurysm?"

"Nope." Mark shook his head, his blue eyes smiling.

Molly left a skewered piece of bread dripping cheese onto her plate. Was Mark being playful with her? To test him, she replied in an exasperated voice, "Intense alien probing."

Mark raised his brows. "I'll give you a hint. It relates to the condition that you mentioned."

"Diabetes?"

"Yes."

"I don't know anything about diabetes, except that you have to take insulin, right?" Molly asked.

"Right."

"So it has something to do with insulin."

Mark nodded. "Now you're getting warmer. Too much insulin, in fact."

"I don't get it."

"He died," Mark told her proudly, "from an insulin overdose."

Molly stared at him. "An overdose? But don't people take insulin using pills or shots? Can you give yourself too much? Explain, please."

"George-Bradley had type II diabetes. People with this condition produce some insulin, but not enough. Or the insulin they produce doesn't work right. You need a certain amount of glucose to keep your body running. Insulin gets the glucose into your cells. Following me so far?"

"Yes, and thank you for putting this into layman's terms for me."

Mark took a breath and continued. "Usually, people who have type II diabetes are middle-aged and overweight. Their cells can't absorb glucose because they don't have enough insulin to let the glucose in, so it's kind of hanging around in their bloodstream. Lots of people with type II can control this by following a careful diet and exercising on a regular basis."

"Something George-Bradley didn't do. He was clearly out of shape, and when I saw him at the kiln opening, he was smoking too. He totally reeked of tobacco."

"So since he didn't maintain a healthy lifestyle he needed to take insulin shots to regulate his glucose levels. Considering he was an overweight smoker, it's amazing he didn't have problems before this."

"How do people know how much insulin to take?" Molly wondered aloud.

"They have portable instruments that measure their blood glucose, or blood sugar levels, as most people say, then they know if it's shot time. Most diabetics can sense when they're in need of insulin. They start feeling weak or dizzy. Some people give themselves shots at regular intervals, like before breakfast and dinner. But diabetes patients can be really different, and there are several different types of insulin. It really depends upon the individual."

"What happens if you get an overdose of insulin?"

"That's called hypoglycemia. Too much insulin makes the body lose its sugar, or its energy. George-Bradley's body just shut down. He was probably comatose before the ambulance even left the garage."

"But I still don't understand. If he gave himself regular shots, how could he give himself too much?"

Mark shrugged. "It's not common, but I guess he could have forgotten that he already had a shot or misread his blood glucose level. By the time that rope was cut, his adrenaline was pumping, he had eaten a bunch of sugary foods, and he had taken a double dose of insulin to boot. I don't know how it happened. All I know is that it was a mistake that cost him his life."

"Wow." Molly tried to absorb all of the medical details. "That's awful. Did you find out anything else?"

"I didn't really ask. I mean all this stuff is confidential, remember? And all you can put in your article is what has been officially released to the press, which isn't much."

"Right. But his cause of death will be made known to his wife and the insurance companies and all that, right?"

"Yes, why?"

Molly wiped the condensation off the surface of her water glass as a thought struck her. "What if it's looked upon as a suicide?"

"Did he seem like someone on the verge of committing suicide?"

"Not at all! He was in his element, according to Mom, and when I met him, he was as chipper as a lark." Molly hesitated, recalling the image of George-Bradley staggering off behind the barn. "The last time I saw him, he was acting dazed. He was rubbing this spot of skin on his stomach. Something was completely wrong about the way he was moving, though. If he had given himself an extra dose, why would he look so surprised about a sore place on his skin?" Molly paused, remembering another detail. "I think I remember a tiny bloodstain on his shirt too. What would that mean?"

Mark dunked a piece of lobster in a bowl of seasoned butter and shrugged. "Sounds like he was examining the spot where he last shot himself. Did you see a syringe?"

"No, but I know he didn't kill himself. Something else happened at that kiln opening."

"Well, then I doubt anyone else will think it's a suicide either." Mark paused, not wanting to offend her. "I'm sure everyone will think that his death was a mistake. Just a stupid, fatal mistake."

Molly thanked Mark for dinner as they parted in the parking deck. She had hoped he would ask to see her again, but then she remembered that they hadn't been on a date, just a working dinner. Tired to the bone, she drove home and phoned her best friend Kitty before turning in.

Kitty and Molly had once taught together at the same private school. For extra money, Molly helped out at Lex Lewis's antique sales as a runner, a clerk, or as floor manager. At a sale when Lex needed another person to help with registration and checkout, Molly brought Kitty along. Sparks immediately flew when Lex and Kitty met, and now they were married and living a few streets away from Clara. They were notorious in Hillsborough as the town's most outwardly affectionate couple. At any given time, one could witness what Clara called "one of their nauseating displays of kissing and pet name calling."

"Chicken!" Kitty screeched the nickname she had given Molly years ago. "What's going on?"

"Girl, you have no idea." And Molly told the story yet again. Kitty wanted every detail, down to what they had to eat for brunch. Because Kitty saw many of the collectors at Lex's auctions, she knew some of the names Molly mentioned.

"That George-Bradley was a regular louse!" she exclaimed, then lowered her voice. "I tell you, every time he came over to my desk to pay after a sale he would just stare at my chest. No shame at all—just stare, stare, and stare. I couldn't stand the man!"

"You don't seem to be alone there. The good news is, I got to discuss the whole event with Mark over dinner."

"THE Mark? Oh, *do* tell."

"It was just a working dinner, nothing romantic. Still, we talked really well together I think."

"Did you talk about anything personal, like does he have a girlfriend?"

Molly hesitated. "No, not really. I did learn today that he almost finished med school but . . ."

"But what?"

"I don't know. I got the feeling that it wasn't a safe subject to discuss. Obviously he dropped out for a reason, and I don't think I should pry."

"Maybe not about that, but you'd better talk to that boy. Now that you've had dinner, the door is open for all kinds of possibilities!" Kitty trilled.

"Oh, do I wish. Anyway, I've got to listen to a message from my editor now, talk to you later."

"I can't wait to tell Lex about the kiln opening. You know he and your mom will be aching to get their hands on that pottery. Sweet dreams of Mark," Kitty said and hung up.

Molly then listened to the rough voice of Carl Swanson rasp out of her answering machine.

"I have another collector for you to see. Hope you've got a pencil," he said as he launched into a wheezing cough. "We're going to run a series on Asheboro collectors. Kind of 'the prime cache of pottery in the middle of the state' theme. Once you're done with the George-Bradley piece, go see a man named Hillary Keane. Yeah, I know, what kind of man's name is Hillary? Sissy. I'll e-mail you his number and address. According to my sources, this guy has an incredible collection. I called him to see if he'd be willing to do the interview, and it's set up for Tuesday at noon. Find out how he got started, where he buys, and photograph his best pieces. We want lots of pictures and he hates having his stuff photographed, so wear something pretty and kiss his butt a little, whatever it takes."

Great, thought Molly as Swanson's voice disappeared. On one hand, there was nothing like interviewing a snob, especially one who wanted to brag about his collection, but didn't want anyone to know too many specifics. On the other hand, Keane had been at the kiln opening *and* George-Bradley had cut in front of him in line. Perhaps this was her chance to begin her detective work.

Molly looked around at her pile of unread mail and sighed. She usually took Sundays and Tuesdays off as she worked Saturdays, but she could see that arguing with Swanson would get her nowhere in view of his current circulation obsession.

A furry body rubbed against her leg, then trotted off toward the kitchen of Molly's tiny house. Molly followed in time to see Griffin jump up to a sitting position on the inside of the dishwasher door. His eyes were large and expectant.

"Oh, now you need a treat, I suppose."

He meowed in agreement.

Rummaging in the fridge, she pulled out a can of whipped topping and made a rippled cream heart on the dishwasher lid. Griffin happily lapped at her design. Molly stared at the flimsy heart and thought of Mark. She wondered if their dinner together had opened the door for other possibilities in his mind as well.

Chapter 5

I say, you look upon this verse,
When I perhaps compounded am with clay,
Do not so much as my poor name rehearse,
But let your love even with my life decay.

—William Shakespeare, Sonnet LXXI

The coffeemaker gurgled and bubbled as the aroma of French vanilla filled the little kitchen. The television was set to the Weather Channel, and Molly missed the local forecast for the third time as she responded to a chorus of cat cries. As she was popping two blueberry waffles in the toaster, the phone rang. Molly knew that a call at this time of the morning could only be from one of three people: her mother, grandmother, or Kitty. She examined her caller ID. It was Clara.

"Hello, Mom."

"How did you know it was me? Oh, that's right, you've got that thing . . . Listen, I have *very* exciting news."

Molly knew from the way her mother's voice dropped to a stage whisper that this news had something to do with antiques or pottery and it was *big*.

"Guess who called me this morning?"

"Grandma," Molly guessed.

"Yes, but guess who *else,*" Clara demanded impatiently.

"Lex."

"Yes!" Clara exclaimed. "And guess who called *him*?"

Molly paused. Who could have sent auctioneer Lex Lewis and her mother into a complete tizzy? After closing her antiques shop, Clara started working part-time at Lex's new auction gallery in Hillsborough. Months later, Lex found he couldn't survive without her and Clara became a silent partner. Though she still ran her own pottery business, Clara found she couldn't bear to sell any of the rare pieces she acquired. Her house became more and more crowded as her "shop" remained rather thin in the inventory department. She put pieces on her Web site every now and then for good measure.

At the auction company, Clara set her own schedule and salary, making up for her lapses in pottery sales. Clara had a good eye for what was saleable and often accompanied Lex when he viewed possible estate sales to help him determine if they would bring in good money.

Someone must have called Lex to look over their goods. Whose house would her mother be chomping at the bit to get into?

"Bunny Staunton?"

"You got it, Madam!" Her mother was bursting. "The funeral is scheduled for Monday, and she already left a message on the auction gallery's answering machine *early* this morning asking Lex to come out and look at the collection."

"The funeral is scheduled for Monday? As in the day after tomorrow? Not next week?"

"Yes."

"And she wants you guys over there today? Isn't this all a bit sudden?" Molly asked incredulously. Funerals were a big thing in the South.

Molly could sense her mother shrugging over the phone. Clara was too distracted to worry about Bunny's motives. Impatiently she replied, "Oh, Bunny must be *dying* to get rid of that pottery. She's always hated the stuff. Get over here this minute! We're leaving at eleven and you don't want to miss it."

Her mother's excitement was contagious. She could see an entire, intact collection of southern pottery before the auction feeding frenzy began.

"No, I don't want to miss it," she assured her mother. "Be right over."

Kitty waited out in the driveway of Clara's house. A traditional North Carolina "shotgun" house, the decrepit structure was on the list of endangered houses when Clara spotted it in her Preservation Society magazine. At the time, she was living in a cookie cutter neighborhood, where every third house was exactly the same except for the shade of vinyl siding. The builder had cut corners wherever possible. The house had looked fine from the outside, but little details like cheap light fixtures, sparse landscaping, and the lack of wainscotings made Clara long for something with character.

When she read that an 1830s farmhouse was soon to be torched as practice for the local fire department, she got right in the car and drove to the site. With her ability to envision the potential in things, Clara knew that her desire for a house with character was about to be fulfilled. She bought the house and its three outbuildings for the mere pittance of $1,500.

Of course, it cost many times that to move it to its new lot in two halves on the beds of two tractor trailers.

Then the chimney was dissembled and reassembled brick by brick, and the log cabin outbuilding recreated by a costly expert.

Surrounded by perennial gardens, tulip poplars, and crepe myrtles, the house looked like it had always belonged on the gentle rise where it peered out upon the passing world. At the time, Molly thought her mother had gone completely mad to embark on such a project, but once it was complete, she was proud that Clara had saved a piece of history and had restored the farmer's home to its simple beauty. It was doubtful, however, that the original owners had as many cats as Clara did.

Kitty was stroking the fur of one of them. The happy creature was named Arthur Ray Cole after one of the area potters. He was a lean, glossy, black cat who rolled on his back with pleasure as Kitty scratched under his chin. Tall and stick thin, Kitty had a cloud of dark, curly brown hair and enormous eyes, light blue as the moonlit snow. When she heard Molly's car, she stood up and waved.

"Hey, Chicken!" she greeted her friend in her high, shrill voice. "Ready to see some stuff?"

"Absolutely. I have my camera too, in case Bunny lets me take some pictures for a future article."

"Lex and your mom are beside themselves. I think we need two bibs for the drooling."

Molly laughed. "Tell me about the message Bunny left."

"It was pretty short and to the point. She said that she heard about Lex doing the deaccession sale for the Mint Museum"—and here Kitty broke out into a very exaggerated drawl and mimicked Bunny's voice—"and I may not know much about *pottery,* but I *do* know *people.* Several of my good friends are *board members* for the museum, so you come *highly* recommended."

"Wow. So then Lex called her back and she wanted him over this fast?" Molly asked.

"She's going to redecorate," announced Lex, hopping down the porch stairs in front of Clara. Lex was a bit shorter than Kitty with close-cropped brown hair and a neat, light brown beard. His chestnut eyes were bright with anticipation. "Right darling?" He grabbed one of Kitty's hands and began planting kisses on it.

"Enough yapping!" Clara quickly clapped her hands and ordered everyone into Lex's van. "Time to go. Hurry, hurry, hurry!"

The Staunton residence was just south of Asheboro, an easy commute to George-Bradley's law office downtown. Driving through the town, it was obvious that the year's drought and bad economy had left their marks on the local businesses. Many spaces were vacant; For Lease or For Rent signs hung in every third window. Most of the stores in operation had large, red Sale! signs in their windows, but these attempts to attract customers did not seem to be working.

The streets were nearly empty. A few people meandered on the sidewalks or looked in windows, but it was very quiet for a Saturday summer morning. The block where George-Bradley's law office was located was tucked away down a side street, but Molly caught the gilt lettering of his sign as the van passed by.

"What do you think will happen to his practice?" she asked out loud.

"He's got a partner," her mother replied, "so I'm sure it will continue under a different name."

Molly mused about the gilt sign. Soon it would be completely replaced and George-Bradley's lengthy name would be erased from the letterhead, the business cards, the legal documents, and slowly, even from memory.

Heading south, Lex drove just outside the city limits and turned right onto a curved lane lined with ancient magnolia trees. They were in bloom; their wide, creamy flowers sat like cupped hands in the waxy leaves. The thick branches met and intertwined across the heights of the street, creating a sun-speckled path to the Staunton Estate.

At the foot of the driveway, two tall wrought iron gates were open for their arrival, controlled electronically from the house. A beautiful cobblestone driveway, slick with water after its wash, led them up a crested hill dotted with dogwoods, pear trees, and crepe myrtles. Each side of the driveway was lined with a bed of lilies, coneflowers, and black-eyed Susans. There wasn't so much as a leaf out of place in the yard. When the house came into view, Molly gasped.

A large Georgian brick, the house greeted them with a wide front veranda bordered by boxwood bushes. Thick, white columns flanked the door and a flagstone path wove off to the side, leading to a walled kitchen garden. From the center of the house, two long wings moved off symmetrically to each side, giving the impression of a pair of strong arms resting on the ground. The beige trim was clean, the black shutters shone as if newly painted, the windows sparkled without streaks in the morning sun, and the front step welcomed them with a woven doormat with the letter *S* monogrammed upon it.

Lex moved forward and rang the bell. A series of ding-dongs purred through the house. Molly half expected a butler to answer the door, stiff-necked and dressed in full house uniform, but Bunny opened it instead.

Bunny looked much like the other wealthy southern women who came to Lex's auctions. She was short and round with plump arms and sausage-shaped fingers. She wore a long, black pantsuit with a chartreuse linen shirt-jacket on top. A thick collar of gold fit snugly around her neck, and she wore several gold bracelets, a Rolex, and rings with large stones on each hand. Her right hand bore a large emerald and her left, a yellow diamond. Her hair was dyed a white blonde that had lost any true sense of color and curled under until it formed a puffed bob. Molly knew instinctively that it was also disciplined into its form with enough hair spray to choke a bull.

Her face was a mask of makeup, including green eye shadow and mauve lipstick. It had been deftly applied and made to look subtle, but in combination with the jewels, the hair, and the strong, musky perfume, Bunny gave the impression that she was just on her way to a high couture fashion show, rather than a widow mourning her husband. However, the expression on her face was all business. Without smiling, she stepped back from the doorframe, allowing them inside. She arched a thin, drawn eyebrow at seeing four people enter when she had only telephoned one.

Lex made the introductions, explaining that his three "assistants" would help him write descriptions of all the objects Bunny was interested in selling. That would enable him to give Bunny a more accurate quote for the auction contract.

Bunny waved his explanation off with an impatient flick of her hand. "I don't need a quote. You're the man for this job, and I'm not concerned about what you get for this stuff, I just want it out of the house."

Her voice was low and humorless. Molly wondered how she was coping with her husband's death. He was a man she seemed to have shared no real passion with. He had cheated on her, filled the house with things she disliked, and avoided her presence. Though Bunny did not look the part of the grieving widow, Molly had a feeling that she was an expert at concealing her feelings when she chose. Were there traces of tension and pain beneath the flat voice and the immovable face?

"M'am?" Molly asked sweetly, already planning ahead for an article on the Stauntons. "Do you mind if I photograph the items you want to sell?"

"Not at all, you will need pictures for the auction anyway, won't you? As far as I'm concerned, you can box it all and get it out of here today."

Lex was unprepared for this. Typically, he went into a residence, looked over the items, then discussed with the owner the probable value, how it should be sold, and what he would charge for his commission. If accepted, he and the other party would sign a contract, and Lex would pack up all of the items to move them to a storage space. If Bunny was offering him items without reviewing the contract right away, they must be low-end or damaged pieces.

"Let's see how much we're talking about." Lex couldn't hide his disappointment. If Bunny was only selling a few pieces of chipped pottery, they had all gotten excited for nothing.

"All of it, naturally. I am going to completely redecorate this wing of the house"—Bunny gestured grandly—"so all four rooms in my . . ." She paused. "That were George-Bradley's can be cleared out."

"Including furniture?" Lex's good humor was instantly restored.

"Everything," Bunny said firmly. "Down to the last paper clip in his desk. I don't want a single item left there, is that understood?"

The four friends were silent. Bunny could not have made it more evident how she felt about her husband. She had hated him. She was getting rid of all signs of his presence, and she was wasting no time about it.

"I understand, and I can take care of everything for you," Lex assured her, which was the perfect reply.

"I'll leave you to it, then." She nodded her head in dismissal and crossed the hall to the other wing, which had been her domain in the divided house.

Clara wisely closed the door leading into the hall, so that the four of them could react to their discoveries without being overheard.

"Wow!" Clara grabbed onto Lex's arm and gave him a shake. "Did you hear what she said?"

"I did!" Lex replied gleefully. "I heard the word *everything*."

The cause for their excitement was obvious, because this room contained valuable antiques. The most eye-catching of them being a large, grandfather clock with a paint-decorated face.

"Walnut," Lex informed them.

"Looks Virginia-made," Clara said as she peered into the face. "Early. It's right, too."

She and Lex exchanged happy looks. Whenever one of them said, "It's right," what they meant was "This is a real antique that has not been damaged or refinished and it will bring a lot of money." But Molly knew it was more than that. Lex and Clara respected a good antique piece. They were harder and harder to find these days, so it was a joy to see something so pristine and graceful, an object of history created with a true craftsman's love and sweat.

Clara had once told Molly that a person could really fall in love with a chest of drawers, a quilt, or a piece of pottery. Molly understood. It was the power of owning something made by hand. These pieces possessed a kind of magic. It was the mark left inside the grains of wood, the strings of thread, or the smooth skin of clay. It held there, fast, through time, and only certain people felt its presence.

Kitty, impatient to get an overview of the rooms, had gone ahead. Now she ran back into the front room, her eyes round with wonder.

"You guys are going to pass out!" She pointed to the rooms down the hall.

But Lex and Clara would not be tempted beyond the living room. They had an 1840s sugar chest to look over, a collection of Chinese import porcelain to view, the weave on an Oriental carpet to examine, and several old oil paintings in gilt frames to inspect. Molly took the hook, however, and followed Kitty's bouncing steps down the hall.

The first room must have been George-Bradley's office. His large, leather-topped desk was the only piece of furniture in the room other than the rows of bookshelves. The shelves covered every open wall and partially obscured both windows. Each shelf held three to seven pieces of pottery. The shelves were perfectly dusted and labeled with a little card that identified the pottery, the maker, and the year purchased. George-Bradley's desk was stacked with a neat pile of reference books on pottery as well as general price guides and books on collecting antiques. Except for last week's Sunday paper, there were no loose papers on the desk surface. George-Bradley clearly liked organization.

Molly looked over the pottery quickly as Kitty was calling her again from the next room. According to the labels, the same potter made most of the pieces, a man named Ben Owen. Molly had heard of him only because her mother had a few of his vases on her dining room mantle. She also knew that his work was strongly influenced by Asian shapes and glazes, and that he made several exquisite vases each year that sold for around $2,000 apiece.

George-Bradley had six of these, standing in a dignified row on two bottom shelves. The glaze was called "Chinese blue," even though it was mostly red in tone with some hints of blue that peeked through in a brilliant shade reminiscent of the Mediterranean Sea.

Clara and Lex appeared in the office.

"My God," her mother breathed. "I have never seen this much Ben Owen in one room."

"Look at these Han vases!" Lex exclaimed. "They're perfect. Think of the money these will bring!"

Clara and Lex were in their element. They showed one another piece after piece, admiring the shape, the shimmers of glaze, and the complete lack of chips or firing cracks.

"He certainly had excellent taste," her mother complimented George-Bradley. "There's not a piece in here that doesn't catch your eye and demand to be looked at."

Molly left Clara and Lex to salivate and continued on to where Kitty waited in the sitting room across the hall. It had a small leather couch and matching wingback chairs turned toward the fireplace. Oriental throw rugs warmed the room in red and blue tones, while English hunting prints raced along the wood-paneled walls. On top of a small hunt board, crystal decanters with sterling silver labels indicated that while gin and vodka were available, the favorite drink was clearly bourbon.

A set of shelves was built into the back wall only. The other walls were given space for a cherry game table and two very old southern stands. Both of the stands held stacks of small, leather-bound books and a collection of carriage clocks, which ticked merrily away as Molly examined the pottery.

"Isn't this your favorite potter?" Kitty asked, holding the figure of a lion out toward Molly.

"Billy Ray Hussey. Yes, it is. I only have one piece, though. Mom gave me one of his cat doorstops for my birthday." She took the lion from Kitty and examined him with wonder. His solid body was glazed a burnt yellow, like the underside of a sunflower petal. His large, brown mane was made from dozens and dozens of individual curls of clay, and his red roaring mouth sported a row of white, pointed teeth.

"Look at that mane." Kitty admired the curls while patting her own. "Kind of looks like mine."

"I read that they call that fur 'cole slaw' in the pottery world. All those little pieces of clay."

"Are you saying that my *fine* hair looks like slaw?" Kitty asked, pretending to be insulted.

Molly smiled, and then pointed to the figure of a poodle with tons of curled clay fired in a white glaze. Kitty showed her a shelf of silly, smiling face jugs, and the women touched the chips of broken dishes that formed the rows of teeth.

"Shall we proceed?" she asked Kitty.

Except for the bathroom, the final room in George-Bradley's wing was a large sunroom with windows overlooking three different views. The outlook to the backyard allowed Molly a view of an immaculately landscaped pool complete with outdoor bar and tables with umbrellas. Beyond the pool she could make out a tennis court nestled in a grove of mature oaks.

"Bunny must've come with a *lot* of money," Kitty observed, in a loud, singsong voice.

"Kitty!" Molly scolded. "Hush!"

The windows directly in front of them overlooked the slope of green lawn leading down to the drive. A gardener was busy weeding one of the beds. His broad back faced the windows, and though Molly couldn't see his face, his muscular arms and baseball cap gave the impression of both strength and youth.

The furniture in this room was simple. There was a long, pine church pew running beneath the windows along the longest wall, an antique music stand, and some kind of wooden box on a side table. Molly moved toward the box and gingerly lifted the lid.

"Kitty, look."

The women stared down at an old, windup music box. Beneath a glass window, five brass bells waited to be rung out by five silver birds whose beaks would delicately peck at them, creating an accompaniment to the song played by the rolling cylinder dotted with raised notes.

"Do we dare?" Molly asked, gazing in wonder at the tiny birds.

"We do," Kitty answered and carefully pulled up the crank that would wind the box.

"Just crank it one or two times, so we can hear a few notes. We don't know how loud it's going to be."

As they watched the cylinder begin to move, the women held their breath. The music began. It was like nothing Molly had ever heard. Sweet notes like trickling water tripped along with the resonating chimes of the birds striking the bells. The sound was light and high, yet reverberated within the depths of the wooden box, creating an echoed base. It was the music of fantasy, of rain falling on the pond's skin, of a butterfly bursting from its chrysalis in silence of the night. It was the hypnotizing language of bees.

Lex and Clara couldn't deny the pull of the music, and the four stood like statues as it moved through them. Molly looked above the box and saw that several old instruments hung from the walls. There was a trumpet, a clarinet, and a flute. On the opposite wall hung a banjo, a tambourine, and a violin.

When the music stopped Kitty whispered in awe, "For such an unpleasant person, he had some wonderful things."

"Professor Plum, with the wrench, in the Music Room," Lex joked to lift the serious mood, his gaze falling upon the old instruments. No one got his joke. "Clue?" he said. "Remember the board game? Oh, forget it."

Undeterred, Clara explained that the shelves covering the back wall were divided into two sections. One half contained the pottery of Jack Graham and face jugs and churns by C. C. Burle. The second set contained fragile roosters by a Georgia family of potters called the Meaders and ovoid jugs from Edgefield, South Carolina.

Encased in glass, one large jug stood aside from the others.

"What's this?" Molly asked her mother.

"That, my dear, is a piece of pottery created by a black man known as Dave the Slave. It's only worth about $20,000."

"Wow," she said picking up an Edgefield crock. "What are these orange stickers on the bottom of each one?"

"Looks like inventory stickers. He must have a master list written up somewhere around here," Clara said.

Molly moved over to the shelves containing Jack Graham's pottery. She immediately loved his work. His vases were small and elegant, fired in crimson reds and deep blues. There were also large vases with wider mouths and fluted rims. Some were swirled in browns and coppery yellows, but others were glazed a cobalt blue and covered with white or yellow drippings. He made large bowls with glazed snakes inside, spiraled and dotted with red curly tongues. Molly reached up and drew down a blue vase with wide shoulders that rose up to a thin, graceful neck.

"Mom," she breathed, "his work is amazing."

Clara watched her daughter's eyes glow in wonder, turning over the vase she held.

"There's nothing like it—to fall in love with something someone else loved to create."

"I can feel it," Molly said softly in embarrassment. "I can feel what he put into this piece."

"I told you," Clara said triumphantly. "Once you've got the bug, you can't go back. Kiss all of your money and your sanity goodbye! Lex, I think you'll have a new bidder at your next sale."

Molly turned the vase upside down and a small piece of square paper fluttered to the ground.

"Looks like a portion of a newspaper article." Molly stooped to retrieve the scrap. "It's been highlighted."

"What does it say?" Clara craned her neck over her daughter's shoulder as Molly proffered the article. It read:

> E.M.—Now, I know you don't make human figurals, but how about animals?
>
> J.G.—No. I stick to pieces I can make by turning.
>
> E.M.—Do you ever think you'll make a figural in the future? How about an experimental cat or a horse?
>
> J.G.—No, I'll leave those for the more talented potters out there. I just never had the notion to make anything off the wheel.
>
> E.M.—Well, if you ever made one I'm sure it would be exceptionally valuable.

"E. M. must be the interviewer and J. G. must be Jack Graham," Molly said. "I wonder why George-Bradley kept this." She then began to examine the bottom of the vase she held. Jack Graham had signed his initials instead of using a metal stamp like most of the other potters. He had also scraped a number into the unglazed clay.

"What's this number?" she asked her mother.

Clara took the vase from her hands. "That's the kiln number. There are fifty to seventy-five pieces of pottery that survive each kiln load. This is an early one. He made this piece, put the number in the clay, and fired the kiln for the fifth time."

"Fifth time ever?" Molly wondered how long ago that was.

Clara nodded. "Yes, from the time he began numbering pieces. I think he made a few kiln loads without numbers first, before he really began selling as a full-time potter. He started off as a welder."

"And he quit his job to make pottery? Did he have any experience?"

"No, he just loved it. It didn't run in his family like it did for most of the other potters. He just tried using the wheel one day and knew he had to learn. Remember what C. C. said, that he had to make pots whether people bought them or not."

Kitty stood over the music stand and thumbed through the large, black book that had rested on its polished surface.

"Hey guys, I think this is the inventory book." She offered it to Lex.

Lex looked over the book's contents. "OK," he said holding it out to them decisively, "first thing we do is check to make sure all these pieces match with everything in this book. He has described every piece down to what riverbed the clay came from, so we already have a great start for the catalogue descriptions."

"When will we pack this up?" Kitty asked.

"We only have a couple boxes in the van. I wasn't prepared to pack. I'll come back on Monday with the big truck and some guys to get it all at once."

"Let's start in the office and work our way back," Clara suggested.

As Lex read from the inventory list, the three women located the pottery and he checked each one off with a pencil.

"Number 3124. A Ben Owen ovoid vase in red glaze."

It should have been easy to find the pottery. The ware was grouped together by maker, the shelves were labeled, and each bore an orange inventory sticker.

"Not here," Clara said, reexamining the shelves. "Maybe he has some upstairs."

"Maybe it's mixed in with some of the other pieces in the other rooms," Kitty offered doubtfully, checking again on the bottom shelves.

After looking through two rooms, including closets, the group discovered that three pieces were missing from George-Bradley's collection.

"Onto the music room," Lex directed.

Checking off from the list, Lex announced that a small Meaders rooster, a Jugtown teapot, and a Northstate vase were missing. That made six pieces in total from the mixed collection.

"Didn't Bunny say all of George-Bradley's saleable items were in this wing?" Clara asked.

"That's what I understood," said Lex.

Molly reviewed the descriptions of the pottery from the inventory book. "They're all smaller pieces," she noticed.

"Maybe they're getting repaired," Kitty suggested.

"George-Bradley was very particular about his pottery," Clara argued practically. "He'd never need to have a piece repaired. He only bought pieces in mint condition."

"Unless the cleaning lady chipped them," Kitty persisted.

"I think George-Bradley was very particular about his pottery." Lex pointed to a feather duster hanging from a hook on the side of one of the shelves. "Those six pieces have to be somewhere else in the house. When we're done with the Jack Grahams, I'll ask Bunny."

The Jack Graham collection was as orderly as the rest. George-Bradley had one or two pieces from every firing from number 1 to number 42. That piece was a long-necked pitcher called a Rebecca pitcher. The next piece, number 44, was a simple, brown shoulder vase, probably the only piece in the collection that seemed to lack personality. Piece number 45 was identical.

"Where's number 43?" Kitty asked.

Lex frowned over the book. "He doesn't have it written down."

"He has every kiln number but that one?" Clara was surprised.

"Must have missed that sale." Lex shrugged. "Let's write a quick list of the furniture and then head out."

"Good, I'm *starving,* honey buns," Kitty whined. Lex put his arm around her waist and gave it a squeeze. As he began whispering endearments in his wife's ear, Clara cleared her throat loudly.

Unabashed, Lex gave Kitty a kiss on the check and declared, "Lunch is on me, ladies. We'll have one of our IHOP specials."

Dreaming of crepes and bacon, cheeseburgers and fries dipped in ranch dressing, and huge glasses of sweet tea, the foursome got back to work.

* * *

They finished up their inventory quickly, driven by hunger and Lex's anxiety to return to the auction gallery to pick a date for what would be one of his finest sales.

"Let me find Bunny to tell her we're done for today."

"Don't forget to ask about the six pieces of missing pottery, sweetie pie," Kitty reminded her husband, blowing kisses at him.

"Oh, I won't, sugar plum," he said sweetly.

Clara rolled her eyes in disgust.

Back in the main hall, the group listened for any stirrings in the rest of the house. The door to Bunny's wing was slightly ajar, so Lex pushed on it while giving a cautionary tap.

"Mrs. Staunton? M'am?"

He knocked a little louder. The sounds of a woman's voice floated out to them. Bunny talked, and then there was a pause, then she talked again.

"She must be on the phone," Molly deduced. "I'll just poke my head in and give her the hand sign that we're leaving."

No one else wanted to go, so her offer was readily accepted. Truth be told, Molly just wanted a glimpse of the other half of the house, knowing she wouldn't be back for Lex's subsequent visits.

She entered the spacious living room, wincing at the bright yellow wallpaper and heavy flowered curtains, getting a glimpse of two plush green chairs facing a yellow-striped sofa strewn with embroidered pillows in yellows, pinks, and greens.

The overdose of color propelled her forward into the hall, but not before she noticed the wedding portrait over the mantel. It was Bunny and George-Bradley, radiant with happiness and expectation. Bunny was gazing at her new husband with a look of pure adoration, a look that Molly had trouble imagining on the present Bunny's face. There were also a dozen photographs lining the mantel. They were all of a happy Staunton couple, taken over a space of twenty years.

Bunny's voice was coming from the furthest room, the one mirroring George-Bradley's music room. Before Molly could announce her presence, Bunny's voice cut through the air.

"But that is *simply* ridiculous!" she yelled in frustration, emphasizing every word. "I told you, he took his insulin *every morning before breakfast*. He took it that morning, I would know because *I* gave it to him." There was a pause as the caller spoke. "He would fill the syringe and hand it to me. No, I don't know how much was in it. I never looked."

This was followed by another pause as Bunny listened to the reply. Molly didn't know where to turn. Her feet were rooted to the ground, curiosity overcoming good manners.

"Look, my husband was very predictable. First the shot, then some coffee, some juice, three eggs over easy, and a side of four pieces of bacon. Every morning for ten years. He hated giving himself the shot and I certainly didn't mind giving it to him. After all, I *am* his wife," Bunny added in a defensive tone.

Bunny paused again, sighing in annoyance.

"Well, that may be, but I'm telling you, he had his morning shot at home!"

Molly heard Bunny slam down the receiver in anger. "Why don't you ask me if I'm glad that my husband had diabetes?" Bunny raged in her office, not knowing that she had an audience on the other side of the door. "Why don't you ask me if I'm glad that he's dead?"

Molly backed quietly out of the hall and coughed loudly once she was standing in the yellow living room.

"Mrs. Staunton?" she called innocently, walking back into the hallway.

Bunny poked her head out of the office door, a manila envelope held protectively to her chest.

"I'm sorry to interrupt you, but I just wanted to let you know that there are a few pieces of pottery listed in George-Bradley's inventory book that aren't on the shelves." Molly talked faster as Bunny stared at her in disinterest. "Could they be anywhere else in the house?"

"No. All of his pottery is in that wing."

Molly shifted from one foot to another. "Do you have a cleaning service?"

Bunny frowned. "We have two wonderful ladies who have been cleaning for me for years. If they broke anything, they'd tell me immediately."

The phone in the office began to ring again. Bunny scowled. "They were probably taken by some of his *collector friends*. They were always dropping by to see his collection, whether he was here or not." She began to turn away, and then paused and added, "And what did I care? I let them in. Now, if you'll excuse me." Bunny went back into her office and shut the door before Molly could ask her the names of these "friends."

Back in the main hall, Lex cocked an eyebrow at her. "You're making a funny face. What did she say?"

"I'll tell you in the car," Molly said, relieved that they were leaving.

The house might be beautiful, but there were some dark

corners where mysteries lurked. Why would a woman who hated her husband keep so many pictures of him near her? Had George-Bradley received his daily insulin shot and then absentmindedly given himself another one? Or had Bunny purposely given her philandering husband an overdose? And where, beyond a house that guarded its secrecy beneath a façade of expensive decorators and immaculate landscaping, were the missing pieces of pottery?

The hands that held the rabbit were not gentle. They were smooth and oily, missing the calluses of work and the coarseness that comes with creation. They were damp, greedy hands that put too much pressure on the clay's hollow neck. Strange smells that were not of the earth, but spoke of dead trees and ink, seeped into the clay's pores, and it protested as the crush of an old piece of newspaper encircled its form.

From its place in the darkness, the rabbit could feel the sway of the man's body. It could smell the odor of stale sweat lining the inside of the cloth pocket, carrying a pungent memory of the compost pile outside of the potter's shed.

The potter's scent was different. Slicked with fresh sweat as he turned, little rivulets of it slipped down his arms and face like rainwater running down a craggy stone. The potter's scent was damp leaves, the hidden skin of pine bark, the soil beneath the cucumber vines, newly sprung mush-rooms, dried moss in the deep wood.

The clay was moving away from its home. It could feel the distance yawning wider and wider. The wheel where it was birthed was gone. The movement was too fast, things passed by in a blur of senses. It could feel the air changing, filling with too many scents of man.

The rabbit was afraid. There were too many noises now. Voices were raised. A woman was shouting, shrilly, like a jay yelling over the ledge of its nest. Lights seeped in through the newspaper but the rabbit felt more than saw the slow movement of shadows. Then it was placed inside another cloth and felt the binding of tape wind around its body. The hands were gone. All was still.

The rabbit could not detect any sound, any sight, any smell. It had been made prisoner within some cave of darkness. There was no hum of the potter's wheel or sounds from his radio. There was no firefly glow from his swinging bulb or the afternoon sunlight leaning in through the shed window like a heavy branch. The other forms of clay, the brothers and sisters, were not here to provide warmth and memory in the night. The clay was lost.

It longed to be back in the riverbed where the darkness was innocent. If it could return to the moist womb of its mother, it could feel the comforting weight of water and see the broken stars swimming above. It longed for escape, to be unknowing, unborn, unmade. But it had lost its power. The man who took it did not hear the calling.

In the darkness, the clay was forgotten.

Chapter 6

Throughout the civilized history of mankind, after the gradual change from nomadic hunter and gatherer to settled farmer and animal breeder, clay has probably been the most consistently used material for improving the quality of life.

—ROBIN HOPPER, FROM *FUNCTIONAL POTTERY FORM AND AESTHETIC IN POTS OF PURPOSE*

On another humid Monday morning, Molly sat in the break room, jotting notes on the Staunton collection. She liked the buzz of peripheral noise as other staffers talked and snacked around the gurgling coffeepot. She needed as much help as possible to shut out the other buzzing in her head—the questions about George-Bradley and his missing pottery.

Clayton, the self-titled Queen of Advertising, marched into the room and sat down across from her.

"Well, Miss Thang," Clayton began, rolling up the sleeves of his silk peach sweater, "I have heard some news about you."

Aside from being the most flamboyant dresser and the bread and butter of the paper, Clayton was an infamous gossip. Molly had exchanged some catty comments with him about their boss, and though Clayton might sling a few verbal barbs around the break room, he was actually a kind-hearted, generous man.

Slicking back his salt-and-pepper hair, Clayton leaned back and examined her. "I do declare, Miss Molly, you have a crush on Mark Harrison."

Molly squirmed in her chair and did her best to look preoccupied with her notepad.

"Don't even try that act with me. You know gay men have supersensitive radar for these kinds of things. Besides, a little birdie told me y'all went to dinner together."

"Oh, Clayton, it was just a working date."

"But you wish it was more, don't you? He is a fine-looking specimen of a man!"

"Shhh!" Molly pleaded in a whisper as another staff member came in. "So you found me out. What are you going to do with this information?"

"Darling! What do you think of me? And why look so glum? If I had your eyes and your complexion, I'd drive straight to Hollywood and demand my own decorating show and I'd get it."

"Thanks, Clayton, but I've got some extra curves you don't have."

"Honey, you've got more curves than a mountain road, but you are fine, fine, fine. Now, I have seen that man looking at you—" He bit off the end of his sentence as Mark entered the room carrying a brown bag in one hand and chopsticks in the other.

"Hi, you two. Care for some Chinese?" he asked.

"A man who eats fatty foods. You are so sexy, Mark Harrison." Clayton twirled Mark's tie around his finger. "Is this a Burberry? Oh, you just get more and more delicious!"

Mark nodded in assent and smiled. "Thanks. Plates for you both?"

"Oh no, not for me!" Clayton trilled. "I've had so many frozen mochas I just can't sit still." He sauntered off, whistling.

"Molly?"

"Sure." She grinned, pleased to be alone with him once again.

As he helped himself to pieces of sesame chicken and steaming white rice, Mark asked Molly what she was working on. She told him all about the visit to the Staunton mansion. She tried to explain how fine the antiques were, but Mark was more interested in the architecture of the house and in Bunny's phone call.

"Whom do you think she was talking to?" he asked.

"I'm not sure. Not a friend. Maybe an insurance agent or lawyer," Molly said.

"Or a doctor?"

"Because of all the extra insulin found in his body?" she asked.

"Yes. There must have been enough extra to catch someone's attention," Mark suggested.

"I still say he'd never overdose on purpose."

Mark frowned. "But didn't you say his marriage was on the rocks?"

"Yes, but it had been that way for years. Why would he commit suicide because of his marriage *now*? And he could just get divorced; he wouldn't have to kill himself. Plus, I think the person who really suffered in that marriage was Bunny."

"Why do you say that?"

Molly told him about the photographs. "It was like she was creating a dream world. She had all these smiling pictures of her and George-Bradley, like they were the perfect couple. Poor thing. Her biggest fault was that she didn't like his stuff. She probably never thought her indifference to his collecting would eventually doom their relationship."

"I do feel sorry for her. Still, she seems to have woken up from her dream world if she's selling all of his belongings this quickly. Seems to have recovered pretty fast, if you ask me."

Molly swallowed a delicious bite of spring roll. "Just in *his* part of the house. I bet, that when she redecorates, she puts up more pictures and creates a kind of mausoleum to their marriage."

"Whatever it takes to get over losing someone . . ." Mark murmured, turning his face away.

Molly sensed that he had suddenly withdrawn but couldn't figure out what she had said wrong. She tried to draw him back by wondering aloud. "But that still leaves the questions of the overdose and his missing pottery?"

"The pottery could be anywhere, and who knows what was going on in his mind the morning he took those shots," Mark said flatly.

"You should have seen how he kept the pottery: all together, labeled, and perfectly dusted. It's missing. I feel it. Do you think his mistress, Susan, ever came in their house? And . . . there's something fishy about the two shots, too. I saw something in George-Bradley's face, Mark. He was surprised in the end. Shocked. You can't easily shock a man like that," she stated animatedly. "There's been foul play, I know it in my gut, and I'm going to try to find out more about all this."

"How?" he asked, looking at her curiously.

"I don't know, but I'm supposed to be doing these articles, so I have reasons to interview people in his circle. I'm going to call some of the suspects from the kiln opening, like Susan Black. It seems that many people hated George-

Bradley, but it just so happens Swanson has me meeting with my first source of inside information tomorrow, twelve o'clock sharp. That's when I will be interviewing a rival collector, a man named Hillary Keane. George-Bradley cut him in line *and* insulted him. He ought to have a lot to say," Molly stated resolutely.

Mark smiled at her stubbornness and laid a tentative hand on her arm. "Just be careful. Curiosity can get you into trouble, especially if you happen to be right and this death is no accident."

Puzzled by Mark's abrupt swings in mood, Molly was nonetheless delighted by his tender smile and the hand on her arm. She felt like it was burning heat right into her.

Molly loved her days off. Usually, Sunday was a day to hang out with Clara and Kitty. Tuesday was the day to spend all morning in pajamas with coffee and a good book. The cats would lie on the sofa with her as she lounged about, reading and watching the Weather Channel.

This Tuesday could not follow the usual pattern. She had her interview with Hillary Keane at noon and needed to fight off her lethargy with a shower and strong coffee.

Her two cats eyed her with disappointment as she came downstairs dressed for the day.

"Sorry, guys." She gave them each a pile of treats. "Mom's got to work today."

The ride to Asheboro was shorter than usual. Molly consulted the directions Swanson had written in his illegible scrawl, and turned off a back road just south of Greensboro. Winding through the countryside, she felt her spirits lift. She was excited about comparing Hillary Keane's collection with George-Bradley's and reminiscing about Mark's face as he touched her arm. She turned up the oldies station she liked, singing along with Elvis to "Viva Las Vegas."

A few miles north of Asheboro, she turned onto a smaller street lined with single-story brick homes and small, two-story bungalows from the 1960s. The lots were large and covered by massive trees and rolling lawns, but the houses were rather dingy and not as well kept as Molly expected. Disappointed, she searched for house numbers, knowing that a ranch-style house could only hold so much pottery.

The last house on the street belonged to Hillary Keane and Molly's hopes were restored. A large white colonial, the house looked down on the street from its green crest and yawned widely with a columned mouth. Surrounded by trimmed rhododendron and azalea bushes, the house looked quite comfortable in its rule over the other homes in the neighborhood. As Molly pulled up the driveway, she admired the large bed of rose bushes to the left and a neat, brick walkway lined with an explosion of impatiens leading up to the front door.

The driveway led her to the back of the house, where a wide, low porch extended out onto the lawn. Molly parked in front of the garage, surprised that it was big enough to hold three cars. She wondered what Keane did for a living in order to afford more than one car and a large pottery collection.

Walking around to the front door, she noticed that the grass was not as neat as the garden beds. Despite the lack of rain, it had grown tall and way overdue for a trim. Molly rang the doorbell and waited, going over her mental checklist of necessary supplies: mini-recorder, pad of paper with questions, pen, and camera. When no one came to the door, she rang again. She could hear the loud bell echo inside the house, but no footsteps came in response.

She decided to try the back door. No answer. She checked her watch. It was exactly noon. Maybe Swanson had set up the wrong day. He had done it before.

Stepping up onto the porch, Molly noticed a pair of parched ferns and a strewn pile of local newspapers around the welcome mat. She picked one up. It was the *Washington Post,* a daily paper. Hillary had left five days worth of papers lying about. Molly frowned. She hated things to be untidy.

Molly opened the screen door and knocked on the wooden one, growing irritated at having given up her day off for no reason. As she stepped back from the door in surrender, a scrap of paper fluttered out from its place between the two doors. She picked it up and read:

Sunday

Hey Buddy,
   Where are you? We had a tea time for this morning.
   Did you forget? Stopped by here to pick you up, but no one was home. I called you on your cell, at home, and at work, but no dice. Let's reschedule for next weekend. Give me a call.

—Gil

Molly stuck the note underneath the grip of the doorknocker, and then peered in one of the porch windows. She could see into the kitchen, where three of the Meaders roosters stood guard from their prominent place on top of the cabinets, but nothing struck her as odd. A mug sat out on the counter next to some brown bananas. Turning back to the drive, she looked again at the papers and the unkempt lawn.

Molly walked over to the garage and tried the door. It was locked. Peering in through the square windows of the garage doors, she could see that only one of the garage bays was occupied. A small, inexpensive pickup truck sat next to an empty bay, while the third was taken up by a large worktable surrounded by tools. Molly assumed Hillary Keane kept his other car in the second bay, so nothing looked unusual in this garage. Except that there were rows of cardboard boxes stacked on shelves lining the entire back wall. Whatever was in those boxes took up a lot of space.

Molly moved over to the far bay, hoping to get a better view of the back wall from a different angle. From this vantage point, she could see that several of the shelves were empty, but still had dust marks showing that boxes had once been there. The box closest to her had obviously been looked at recently, because the newspaper had not been completely replaced. No longer in hiding, the necks of two large pottery jugs jutted out from their nest. The rows and rows of packed boxes all contained pottery!

But why would Hillary Keane keep all his pottery out here, out of sight? Pottery collectors loved to touch and see their objects of desire. How had Keane planned to show *her* his collection if it was all buried out here in the garage?

She walked back toward her car and dialed the office. Swanson's secretary informed her that he was home with a cold and gave her his home number. She knew that there was a good chance her "sick" boss would be out fishing, but he answered his phone with an angry grunt.

"Carl? It's Molly."

"This better be good," he grumbled. "I've got a nasty cold, you know."

"Sorry to hear that. I'm at Hillary Keane's house, for our appointment, but he's not here."

"And what would you like me to do about that?" Swanson demanded.

"I'm just checking to make sure this is the right day," Molly said carefully.

"Of course it is!" he barked. "I talked to him on Thursday, the day before the Burle kiln opening. He said he was thrilled to be able to show off his collection. Really wanted to help spread the word about the local potters. Seemed like a decent guy, for a snob."

"Well, maybe he had to leave town. What should I do now?"

Swanson sighed, "I'll call my friend and see if he knows what happened to Keane."

"His name wouldn't be Gil, would it?" Molly asked.

"No, it's Bryant. Why?"

"He was supposed to play golf with Gil on Sunday. There's a note here from his friend."

Uninterested, Swanson replied, "That's where I'm going right now. I need *something* to get my mind off of this cold."

Molly hung up and returned to her sweltering car. As she backed down the driveway, the house stared down at her through the streaked sunlight. It seemed especially silent on its lonely hill. Molly suddenly remembered how George-Bradley had cut in front of Keane at C. C.'s kiln opening. The look of outrage in Keane's eyes was unforgettable. Had George-Bradley stepped on Keane's toes more than once? Molly had a strong feeling that something was wrong in Hillary Keane's life, and it wasn't some sick grandmother. One thing she felt with conviction. Whatever had caused Hillary Keane's absence had something to do with pottery.

On the ride home, Molly called her mother to see if she wanted to go out for dinner. Clara was settled in a lounge chair reading. She sat up lazily and reached for the phone; only her interest in hearing about Hillary Keane's collection could tear her away from the mystery she was reading.

"How's Lord Menes doing?" Molly asked after the novel's hunky Egyptian hero. She had already plowed through the series of five books.

"Handsome as ever. Every other paragraph is about his muscular, tan torso. I can't stand it."

"What will you do once you're finished?"

Her mother sighed longingly. "I'll just have to reread all the Horatio Hornblower books to keep me satisfied. How was your interview?"

"Didn't happen."

"What do you mean?"

Molly told her mother about her visit to Hillary Keane's. Clara listened, frowning in thought.

"In cardboard boxes?" she asked, completely perplexed. "What's the point?"

"Maybe he just liked to hoard stuff. My boss said he sounded like a nice enough guy when they talked on the phone," Molly said.

"It's the South. Everyone sounds nice and polite on the phone. Doesn't mean they can't bite like a dog at any other time."

"True, but I may never find out. Carl is checking it out and will call me back tonight."

"What are we doing for dinner?" Clara leaned back in her lounge, her long, tan legs stretched out. "It's too hot to cook. Let's go to Panchos."

Molly laughed. "Excellent idea. I could use a margarita. After all, this *was* my day off."

Panchos was one of the few restaurants in Hillsborough. It had had a slow start, locating to a town where people had been eating grits and barbeque all their lives. But it hadn't taken long for the delicious and inexpensive Mexican food to seduce the taste buds of even the least risk-taking eaters in town.

Molly and Clara ordered grande margaritas and dug into the warm tortillas and spicy salsa.

"Time to talk about serious matters," Molly began, swallowing a sip of her frozen delight. "There is something rotten in the state of North Carolina."

"Such as?"

Molly pushed the basket of chips toward her mother. "George-Bradley's death, for starters. Bunny was adamant that she gave him his daily insulin shot. On top of that, there's the missing pottery."

"Lex is going back over to the Staunton place tomorrow. He'll ask the cleaning lady if she knows anything and one mystery will be solved. As for the insulin issue, what are you getting at?"

"What if someone *gave* him more insulin? Someone who knew he had diabetes and knew his habits well enough to know that he'd already had one shot."

"So you're still suggesting *murder*?" Clara asked loudly.

At that awkward moment, the waitress arrived to take their orders. Her mother chose a vegetarian plate with bean burritos and cheese enchiladas. Molly skipped the beans and went for three cheese enchiladas.

"I need my calcium," she told the waitress sheepishly. Turning back to her mother, she answered, "Yes, I am."

"Who would be your suspects?"

As a plate of sizzling fajitas passed them by, Molly suggested that either Bunny or Susan would be the obvious killer.

"I don't know," Clara pondered. "Susan seemed to dislike him so much lately. I don't even think she'd want him back as a boyfriend. Why kill him? I think Bunny had more reason to do that."

Molly rubbed salt from the rim of her glass. "But what about all of those pictures Bunny had of them together?"

"That doesn't mean *anything*," Clara said dismissively. "Those could totally be there for show. Bunny wouldn't let it *seem* like they were anything but happy."

"She was pretty clear about how she felt when we were there."

"That's because *we* don't count as people who matter. We're the *help*."

"So what about Hillary Keane's anger at the kiln opening? Keane knew George-Bradley, I could tell by the look he gave our victim. And what about Keane blowing off both my interview and the friend he was supposed to play golf with? The man is gone, I tell you."

"He had to leave town. He'll turn up. Look, as much as I love a good mystery, I don't think there is one here."

As the waitress arrived with scalding plates of food, Molly's phone chirped from within her purse. She quickly grabbed it and made for the door. It was a pet peeve of hers that people had loud phone conversations in restaurants, and she vowed never to be so impolite.

"Hello?"

Her boss coughed in her ear. "Seems that Keane really has disappeared. He hasn't been to work for the last couple of days and my friend hasn't heard a word from him either. Says the two of them are pretty close, too. He's actually going to call the police. In the meantime, why don't you interview that potter who used to visit your school? You told me about him last year."

"Oh, Sam Chance! I would love to see him again." Molly was thrilled. Swanson was lining up another person who had been to the kiln opening. However, she thought of one drawback. "But you know, Sam makes mostly functional pottery. Nothing fancy."

"That's fine. We want to represent a varied mix of potters. It's not like people don't collect dishes . . ."

"True. I'm also hoping to line something up with Susan Black, another collector. I left a message on her answering machine, but haven't heard anything yet . . . Listen, is Keane married?" Molly asked.

"Nope, he's a bachelor, unlike me. And my wife is calling me for supper."

"Wait!" Molly caught him. "Just tell me one more thing. What is Keane's profession?"

"He's a pharmacist."

Molly snapped her cell phone closed and rejoined her mother.

"I've got a new suspect to add to my list," she told Clara proudly.

"OK. According to you, we have Bunny the jealous wife, Susan the vengeful mistress, and now . . . ?"

"Hillary Keane," Molly announced.

"What did your boss say?" Clara asked.

"Keane has officially gone missing. Hasn't been home, hasn't been to work, and no one seems to know where he is. The police are being called in to investigate."

"And why does that make him a suspect?"

"Because of his job. He's a pharmacist!" Molly exclaimed.

Clara sat back in her chair and sipped her drink thoughtfully. Then her eyes widened. "He's got access to insulin."

"Exactly. And maybe he gave himself *access* to some of George-Bradley's pottery. That could explain the *where* in our 'where has the pottery gone?' question."

"Fine, say Keane wanted to knock off George-Bradley and take some pieces, how would he give him the extra insulin? I saw him at the kiln opening, but only for a moment."

"I don't know. I'd have to ask Mark for some ideas."

Clara's glass stopped in midair on the way to her mouth. "Mark?"

"Oh, he's a coworker." Molly tried to keep from blushing, but Clara sensed there was more to be discovered about this coworker.

"What would your coworker know about diabetes?" she asked.

"He went to med school for three years. He knows a lot," Molly defended Mark, and then quickly got off the subject. "Back to Keane."

Clara put up her hand to stop her daughter from continuing. "If Keane *had* stolen pottery he could never put the pieces on display."

Molly jerked her fork in the air. "Thus the boxes in the garage!"

Clara was still doubtful. "That would be an awful lot of stolen pieces. Someone would know."

"Maybe he was selling them."

"That's possible." Clara thought for a moment. "He could be selling up north where people wouldn't know whose collection the stuff came from. But he couldn't use an online auction or anything like that; people around here would recognize the pieces."

The two women mused over their theories. Riddles circulated like pesky summer flies.

"The real question is"—Molly paused for emphasis—"Who would know what the relationship was between George-Bradley and Hillary Keane? If one of them bore a grudge against the other, maybe we can link this all up."

"I'll call Donald." Clara signaled the waitress for the check. "He knows everyone who collects pottery. If anyone knows about a connection between George-Bradley and Keane, he will."

Without a doubt, Clara's friend Donald had the largest and most valuable southern pottery collection of the region. His collection was even larger and more valuable than George-Bradley's. Unlike his former rival, Donald also supported the potters in other ways besides buying their wares. He helped them to market their pieces and even lent them money to open their own shops after completing an apprenticeship.

Donald attended almost every area kiln opening, bought at auction, and made deals with other collectors. His trade was in the jewelry business, but his real love was pottery. He and Clara had met over ten years ago at a sale and had become fast friends. Now they helped one another track down unusual pieces for their collections and often invested in pieces together that were later sold at the region's largest pottery show for a nice profit. When Donald wasn't selling jewelry, he was out "beating the bushes" for pottery. He knew everyone who owned so much as a clay ashtray.

"Will you call tonight?" Molly asked hopefully.

Clara looked at her watch. "No, it's too late. It will have to wait until tomorrow. By then, Lex will have found out if the pottery is somewhere else in the house and maybe we can tie up some loose ends."

"I'll have to settle for tomorrow then," Molly sighed, getting up. On the way to the car she put her arm around her mother's waist and squeezed. "But just think, Mom. If we could solve this mystery I could write the best article *Collector's Weekly* has ever seen. It would make my earlier pieces about ghost bidding and online fraud look like small change!"

Chapter 7

Molly was scrubbing the bathtub when the phone rang. She turned off the water and grabbed the receiver, water dripping down her arm and onto the carpet.

"Hello?" she asked abruptly.

"My, my, aren't we crabby? And what are you doing home on a Wednesday?"

"Oh, sorry, Mom. I was just cleaning the bathroom. Can you hold on for a sec?" Molly peeled off her yellow rubber gloves and wiped her arms on the bath towel. "I'm using the time I wasted yesterday to clean house and run errands. What's up?"

"Lots, and it cost me lunch."

"You saw Donald today?" Molly asked.

"Yes. I took him to his favorite Chinese place and mercilessly pumped him for information." Clara laughed mischievously.

"And?"

"Well, he didn't want to tell me anything at first. Hillary, George-Bradley, all these guys grew up together you know, so they don't like telling stories about one another."

"Even to you? You guys gossip about everyone."

"I know, that's why it was strange that he was so reluctant, but don't worry, I finally got some juicy tidbits from him." Clara paused to bait her daughter.

"Go on!" Molly prompted excitedly.

"Well, back in the early days of George-Bradley's collecting, he and Keane used to go to kiln openings and auctions together. They knew each other back in junior high, drifted apart during college, and were kind of reacquainted through pottery. Problem was, they both liked the same pieces. George-Bradley could afford them. Keane could buy sometimes, but more often than not, he had to watch as George-Bradley bought up all the best pieces."

"So he began getting jealous."

"Yes. But according to Donald, it took a few years to bubble to the surface. From the outside, you'd never know that those two weren't the perfect buddies. They went to one another's parties, traveled to shows out of state together, and were generally thought to be best friends."

"What happened?"

Clara sighed. "This is the part where Donald got fidgety. Apparently, Keane started dropping by George-Bradley's house when he wasn't home. He would tell Bunny that he would just wait in the living room. Sometimes he *was* still there when George-Bradley got back, but other times, he wasn't."

"Because he was stealing pottery!" Molly exclaimed.

"That's what George-Bradley thought too. He noticed a piece missing after one of Keane's visits.

"Donald was at a swank party given for members of the

Southern Pottery Collector's Group when he overheard the two friends go at it. George-Bradley accused Keane of taking some of his pieces while he was out of the house—pieces that Keane had always coveted."

"Did Keane make a scene?"

"Not really. Donald said Keane got really red in the face and told George-Bradley in an outraged whisper that their years of friendship obviously meant nothing if he was being called a thief by the one man he thought of as a *brother.*"

"How dramatic."

"Exactly. George-Bradley didn't bother apologizing. They just stared at one another. Then Keane downed his drink and left the party."

"But they still must have run into each other all the time after that."

"Donald says you couldn't tell they even knew each other from the way they acted. He only knows the truth because he was standing close enough to them to hear their argument."

"How long ago did they stop being friends?" Molly asked.

"A couple years ago."

Molly tried to picture the scene at the party. "So after he stopped bumming around with Keane, George-Bradley started finding women to accompany him to sales and shows instead?"

"I guess."

"Well, there you have it. He's a suspect!" Molly declared. "However, there's a detail that I need to find out to confirm my suspicions."

Clara cleared her throat. "What's that?"

"Well, I've been thinking. Mark told me that George-

Bradley suffered from an overdose at the kiln opening. But I wonder, with all that sugary food, *plus* sweet tea, wouldn't he have had enough sugar to balance out the insulin even if he gave himself an extra dose? If he *had* taken two shots, he must have had the second one well before he arrived and ate all that sugar."

Clara considered this. "So you need to find out where George-Bradley was before the kiln opening?"

"If he was only with Bunny then she's my number one suspect," Molly continued. "Though it's pretty suspect that Keane flew the coop right after George-Bradley's death. Perhaps Keane and Bunny were in it together," Molly added, though she didn't really subscribe to this theory. "She hated the pottery. He coveted it."

Clara ignored the latter bits of her daughter's speculations. "You'll have to ask Bunny if George-Bradley was home right up until the time he left for the kiln opening. I don't know *how* you'd bring that up in conversation with her."

"Me either," Molly confessed. She thanked her mother and then dialed Mark's extension at the office.

"I am *so* glad you're in," she gushed when he answered.

"Wow, thanks," Mark replied happily.

"I've got a medical question for you."

"And here I thought just the sound of my voice made you weak in the knees," he teased.

Molly took a deep breath and confessed, "It does," then quickly stammered, "Uh . . . listen, if George-Bradley had taken two shots of insulin, would a pile of cookies and some sweet tea negate the overdose?"

"Depends on how much extra insulin we're taking about. It could certainly slow down any negative side effects—enough to get him to the hospital for treatment."

"So that's a 'yes?' "

"It depends on how many units he took with each shot. If that second shot were a much higher dose, there'd be a bigger risk of death."

"And who would know how many units he regularly took besides his doctor?" Molly asked.

Mark paused to think. "His pharmacist, I guess."

"His pharmacist," Molly repeated.

"Are you still playing detective?" he asked playfully, and she related all of her suspicions to him while trying not to sound like a fool.

"The biggest holes in my theories are how would Keane give George-Bradley the extra insulin?" she asked, grateful that Mark was taking her seriously. "And why now? Did he want to steal more pottery? Was he having money problems?"

"George-Bradley took a shot to get his insulin. I'd think he'd notice if someone stuck him with a needle," Mark pointed out.

Realization hit Molly on the head like a flying brick. "But that's exactly it!" she shouted excitedly. "That's why he was rubbing his stomach. He wasn't doing that because he had just given himself a shot. Bunny always did that for him at home. No . . . someone stuck him at the kiln opening! There was such a rush of people bumping into one another . . . it was the perfect opportunity. Keane was there, and *he* has access to insulin."

"Molly, it would have to be a *huge* dose to cause the reaction that it did. Do you have any other evidence?"

"Not yet. I'm going to interview my friend Sam Chance tomorrow. I'll see if he knows anything we don't know about George-Bradley or Hillary Keane. Plus, he was at the kiln opening and he always has his ear to the ground."

"Is he a potter or collector?"

Molly smiled over the phone. "A potter and one of the nicest people I've ever met."

"Have a good trip," Mark said warmly. "And let me know if . . . um . . . if you get stuck . . . I could be your Watson."

"Well, Doctor," Molly replied coyly, her heart singing, "you may just get the job."

Chapter 8

Chance's Ware was in Seagrove, off the beaten path. Molly had plenty of time to spare, so she took a detour before her interview. Donald had told Clara over a bowl of steamed dumplings that Keane worked at the pharmacy downtown. That could only mean downtown Asheboro. Molly looked in the phone book and discovered only two pharmacies within city limits. She figured she could find the right one.

Her plan was simple: find out exactly when Keane took off and if anyone had noticed him acting strangely. She planned to pretend to be a friend delivering a piece of pottery who hadn't heard a thing about Keane's disappearance. Molly had a weak poker face, so she prayed she could carry this off or her detective work would meet a quick end.

The closest pharmacy was a small brick building on the corner. Urns of pink petunias turned their faces up to greet the rays of sun bouncing off the store windows in a wash of white light. The parking lot was swept clean and a little bell trilled out her arrival as she opened the paneled door.

She spotted a red and white sign reading Prescriptions in the back of the store. A girl who looked as though she should be in high school filed orders into alphabetical bins. She crackled bubble gum in time to the jazzy elevator music, blowing large, pink balloons and then sucking them back into her mouth with a series of snaps and pops. Her dirty blonde hair, held back in a ponytail, swung back and forth like a pendulum as she moved from bin to bin.

Molly took a breath and approached her. "Excuse me."

The girl swung around, her hair whipping over her shoulder. Her name tag read Brandy.

"Yeah." She looked at Molly blankly.

"I'm looking for Mr. Keane," she said in her most sugary voice.

Brandy's eyes immediately narrowed and her jaw froze midchew. "He's not here," and then she added reluctantly, "Can I help you with somethin'?"

"No," Molly assured her. "I've come to deliver a piece of pottery to him."

"Sorry, he's not in," the girl replied flatly.

"But we were supposed to meet today," Molly insisted gently.

Brandy digested this bit of information while indecision played across her freckled face.

"Look." Her voice became strained. "He hasn't been to work for over a week. I don't know what else to tell you."

Molly dropped her eyes to the counter and frowned, doing her best to act worried. "Is he OK?"

The conspiring whisper and the concerned face drew

Brandy in. "We don't know," she admitted, leaning closer. "He's *missing*."

"What?" Molly asked breathlessly, looking around the room wildly, hoping she wasn't overacting. "Since when?"

"Friday afternoon, I guess." The girl closed up again. She obviously cared for her boss on some level and wasn't willing to expose her feelings to a stranger.

Last Friday had been the day of the kiln opening. Molly swallowed her excitement. She reached across the counter, patted the girl's forearm, and replied tenderly, "You poor thing. You must be worried sick."

Brandy's face broke open. "I am," she confessed. "I worked with him that afternoon. He took the morning off to go to some pottery thing. I was the last one to see him."

"You must have to get in here awfully early," Molly sympathized.

"Yeah, 'bout 7:00 to get all the orders ready by openin' time," she sighed. "The cashiers don't have to be here 'til 8:30, but *we,* I mean, Mr. Keane and me, we gotta be here early every single day."

"Do you always have the same shift?" Molly asked, an idea forming.

Brandy blew an enormous bubble and sucked it back into her mouth as she studied Molly. "Yeah. There's a pharmacist's assistant who works evenings, but he works by himself."

"You and Mr. Keane must be close, working side by side every day . . ." Molly suggested. She was hoping that showing a willingness to listen would get Brandy to confess something more intimate about her working relationship. Her intuition paid off.

The girl hesitated and her shoulders slumped. Finally,

she said very softly, "We are. He hired me after I got . . . after I had some trouble. Not many people would do that. I really need this job."

"He is a good man," Molly agreed with false enthusiasm. She suddenly felt guilty about pumping this girl for information. She might look young and innocent, but she had clearly had to grow up swiftly. Now her benefactor had disappeared, and the town was probably rife with rumor.

"Look," she said brightly, trying to ease the girl's mind, "maybe he took a last-minute trip to get away from it all . . . did he seemed stressed to you?"

The girl shook her head, her mind elsewhere.

"Well, these pottery people are always running off to some show or another." She felt another pang of guilt. "Did he act like he was excited about something or . . . maybe worried about something?"

Brandy looked at her like she was the village idiot. "He's always worried! He has a good reason to be!"

What did that mean? Suddenly, an image flashed before Molly's eyes. She remembered Keane at the kiln opening, struggling to clean his glasses. Those hands. They had been so gnarled and his face had been filled with embarrassment and frustration. Molly had seen hands like that before. Her grandmother's sister, an accomplished pianist, had developed such bad arthritis in her early sixties that she could no longer play. Molly recalled a faint memory of the swollen knuckles, the disobedient fingers, and the embarrassed flush on her great aunt's face as she attempted to peel an apple over the sink.

"Of course," Molly whispered, more to herself than to the girl. "What pain he must have been in all the time."

Brandy responded to the genuine sympathy in Molly's voice. "He was. Even though he takes medicine, he can hardly open any bottles anymore." She looked around to make sure no one could hear. "I have to use all the keys for him. It's too hard for him to hold onto them. It's not fair, either. It's not like he's an old man, but he has such an advanced case."

Molly realized that Brandy was at least a little bit in love with her employer. "It's good of you to help him," she said kindly. "He helped you, so now you keep his arthritis a secret. You make it so that he can still do his job."

But Molly had gone too far in revealing Keane's affliction. Brandy gave her an icy stare, mumbled, "Yeah," and returned back to her work and defensive gum chewing.

"Look, if I hear anything about him, I'll call you," Molly offered, even though Brandy had turned away. "No matter what, you'll be just fine. You obviously have a good head on your shoulders."

Brandy raised her face and gave a slight nod. Molly retreated to her car, feeling like a complete jerk. Her theory about Keane had been shot to bits. If he had such an advanced case of arthritis that he couldn't open a bottle cap or turn a set of keys, there was no way he could squeeze the tiny syringe used to give George-Bradley the extra shot of insulin. But if Keane was innocent of the murder, why had he run away?

Molly stopped to pick up a dozen donuts. Sam Chance loved anything with sugar, and his apprentices were always hungry. Consulting her Seagrove area potteries map, she remembered that the closest landmark to Chance's Ware was the abandoned Chance Beans factory. The dilapidated building and overgrown land proudly displayed a real estate sign. Molly was surprised to see that the sign read Sold.

Chance's Ware was down a long, gravel road, much like a hundred other potters in the area. The yard seemed deserted but for the new Ford pickup resting under a carport.

"Someone has a new truck." She greeted Sam with a hug as he came out of the workshop.

His kind face broke out in a wide grin, scattering laugh lines across his cheeks and scuttling creases into the corners of his blue eyes. "Yes, indeed." He rocked back on his heels, hands tucked into his overall pockets as they admired the sheen of the vehicle.

"Did some Chance Beans relative leave you a pile after they sold their land?"

"Now you know I'm no kin to them. If I were, I'd be messin' around with clay for fun and wouldn't trouble over sellin' a pot. Nope," he said as he patted the hood of his truck affectionately, "bought this by sweat and tears."

"Brought y'all something to cure your sweet tooth," Molly said as she handed him the box of donuts.

"Oh boy," Sam whistled. "This'll help, but my case is hopeless. Come on up to the shop."

They reached the metal-sided barn, which housed Sam's wheel, drying shelves, glaze barrels, and all the ware for sale. Molly looked around at his utilitarian ware. He made plates, bowls, pitchers, candleholders, bean pots, casseroles, and birdhouses in four different glazes. His traditional pieces were concentrated on a single table where several face jugs with corncob stoppers and a few roosters proudly proclaimed their creator's right as a fifth-generation potter.

"So what do you want to cover today? Lord knows I could talk pottery to ya until the cows come home, but I don't figure you've got all that much time."

Molly watched as Sam helped himself to a jelly donut.

"How about digging the clay and turning. Unless you want to talk about firing too."

"Well, you've been to C. C.'s," Sam said, "so you've seen the best kiln around these parts. He's got the genuine article in that groundhog kiln of his."

"Let's cover how a piece of wet clay becomes a jug," Molly suggested.

"All the action before glazing."

"Right."

Sam dusted sugar particles from his overalls, pointing to a shelf of unglazed pots. "It's called bisque-ware when the pottery hasn't been glazed yet. Lots of us say 'biscuit' for short."

"If it sounds like food, then I can remember it." Molly accepted a chocolate-frosted donut for herself. "Where are all your apprentices today?"

"Oh, they're delivering a load to some gardening place in Asheville. Lady bought up all my flower pots and bird-houses except this one."

"That's great, Sam! And where's your talented son Justin, the famous sixth-generation Chance potter?"

A look of sadness surfaced in Sam's eyes, then darted away like a startled minnow. "He's going to law school."

"Oh. What does that mean?"

"Well, he's using the kiln at the university's main campus, so he hasn't quit pottery. But I don't think he's going to be a full-time potter. I can only hope that I live long enough to wait for him to retire from the law and take over the business."

Molly reassured her friend with a pat on the hand. "Maybe he just needs to spread his wings for a few years. He'll end up here eventually."

Sam smiled, his good humor restored. "I hope so, because we're a dying breed out here."

Sam led her down to the banks of the creek that snaked through long grasses and stooped trees. There, a large, depressed circle formed a wide bog. Molly poked at the clay with a stick and asked Sam if he had stayed at C. C.'s long enough to see the collapse of George-Bradley.

"I sure did. The whole town is a-twitter over it. It's a shame, him being so young and all."

Calling George-Bradley young was a stretch, but Sam always had a kind word for everyone. Molly knew that George-Bradley wouldn't have bought much from Sam because he wasn't as collectible as many of the other potters, but it didn't affect the potter's disposition. But then, Molly suddenly remembered how rude George-Bradley had been to Sam at the kiln opening, slighting him for creating "pretty dinner plates" instead of traditional art pottery. Was it possible that Sam wanted revenge for having his life's work insulted so publicly?

"Weren't you mad at him for what he said to you that morning?" Molly watched Sam's face carefully as he replied, even though she didn't really believe Sam had the capacity to hurt anyone.

"Shoot." Sam shook his head. "I can't get in a huff just 'cause some big shot doesn't like what I make. Those dinner plates have sent my two boys to college, and we've had full bellies every day of our lives." He grinned nonchalantly, rubbing his small pouch.

"Now, back to business. This is our clay pit." He pointed at the bog. "We dig it, mix it up with some commercial clay, and add some water. That gives it a good, plastic feel. You gotta have that to turn."

"I bet you get some serious mosquitoes from that pit." Molly felt itchy just looking at it.

"I wear overalls for more than one reason," Sam laughed, leading her back toward the shop where he pointed at a square machine the size of a refrigerator turned on its side.

"This is a motorized pug mill. It mixes the clay. Back in my Daddy's day, they had a pug mill turned by a mule. Most people had those kind, but none of us keep mules anymore."

"Does this do a better job?"

"Not really, but we just got sick of puttin' that poor mule to work. Us kids were all crazy about that mule. She was our family pet." Sam rocked back on his heels, remembering.

"So she retired and lived a good life?"

"Not exactly. We stopped working her, and just about her first day off she keeled over and died on us."

"That's a terrible story!" Molly laughed. "What did you call her?"

"Whiskey Girl. Whiskey jugs were real big when my Daddy was turning. Everybody wanted one, especially with our corncobs stuck in 'em. So it seems like we heard that word about a million times a day."

Molly made a mental note to add the mule story to her article. "So what's next, after the clay gets mixed up?"

"Well, now you've gotta pick the junk out of it. You're gonna have all kinds of stuff in there. Stuff the screens don't get out. So you need to cut it up into slabs and pick it out."

Sam picked up a block of clay and sliced into it with a wire.

"Banjo string," he told her, cutting a bread-sized piece of clay that revealed embedded pieces of grass and stone.

"May I?" Molly helped herself to a slab and pulled out the invasive bits of nature. The clay was cool and moist, nestling comfortably in her hand.

"Now you've got to get it ready for the wheel. That means a good beating."

Molly jumped as Sam slapped their combined pieces onto the worktable. He picked up the mass, pushed it together, and slammed it down again and again.

"That looks positively therapeutic," Molly said.

"It helps after a weekend of not selling a single thing."

Once the clay was worked into the right plasticity, Sam slapped it on the wheel.

"This is the hard part." Sam gestured to her to approach the wheel. "Give it a try."

He issued instructions on how to use the foot pedal, and as she pushed down on it the wheel sprung into action, and the clay mass lunged sideways, seeking a means of escape.

"Whoa, slow down there," Sam laughed, easing her foot off the pedal. "Now let's give this guy a shower."

Molly cupped the clay lightly in her hands as Sam drizzled it with water. As she spun the wheel, it moved through her fingers like the smooth back of a snake.

"Now, you can't go gentle with it. Gotta treat it like a spoilt child due for a lickin'. Cup it hard with the insides of your palms, I'm gonna help you center it."

Sam guided her hands and touched places on her forearms where she needed to use some sleeping muscles to coax the clay to the center of the wheel. Molly was surprised at the strength it took to force the clay against its will to move from the spot where it was placed originally. Now she understood why all the potters had arms like Popeye the Sailor.

"Good. Now I'm gonna open it up for you."

Sam leaned over the opposite side of the wheel with a tool comprised of a board with a metal ball in the middle. He pressured the ball into the top of the clay's mass, and an open mouth sprang into the clay's center, yawning crookedly as Molly tried to control the body with one hand and widen the mouth with the other. Her novice hands were no match for the clay. It bucked and kicked out like a rodeo pony, and she grew frustrated as she tried to bring it under the rein of her palms.

"This is *hard*," she said, forcing out a laugh. She was disappointed that she didn't have more skill.

"Yep. Takes years to really figure it all out. How does the clay feel?"

"Like it's alive. It sure has a mind of its own. I kind of respect it. But I'm mad at it too, for not doing what's in my mind's eye."

Sam chuckled. "Well, that's your first lesson. You don't *think* when your hands are on the clay. You let go—your body moves its body."

Molly watched in a semihypnotic state as Sam pulled up her floppy bowl into an oblong shape and closed up the mouth into a thin neck. His hands moved slowly, with deliberate grace, and the clay immediately recognized him and fell obedient.

"Let's put a handle on," he said.

Sam showed her how to slice a strip of clay for the handle. After he applied it to the jug, he slipped wire under its bottom and picked it up with large, wooden tongs that reminded Molly of men moving ice blocks one hundred years ago instead of a wet, fragile vessel in the southern summer.

"Wanna make a face?" Sam asked.

"Sure, how about a devil?"

"We'll have to let the jug dry a bit first. Come on into the house and I'll show you my collection."

They gave their hands a cursory washing in the rain barrel and moved on up to the large log cabin nuzzling a grove of pines. Sam's collection was held in the front room. He showed her face jugs from his father and grandfather's time, and other family pieces dating before the Civil War. The greenish glaze, flaked with imperfections, was the same he used. It looked much like C. C.'s, which made sense since both men worked together as apprentices when they were young.

On another bookcase, Sam had collected various pieces from other Seagrove potters. Molly recognized a Billy Ray Hussey lion and a water pitcher made by the Cole family, but the shelf of Jack Graham pieces immediately drew her attention away from all the others.

"I think he's wonderful," she said, admiring a crimson vase.

"These are early ones." Sam tilted the vase upside down to show her the kiln number. It was from kiln number 5. That would be way back in the early eighties."

"You must have been at the same openings as George-Bradley. I just saw his collection."

Sam nodded. "Oh sure, he'd never miss a Jack Graham sale."

"He missed number 43," Molly said.

Sam frowned, looking down on his collection. "I don't have any from that kiln opening either."

Molly started. Here were two men who never missed a Graham kiln opening, yet neither one had made it to the number 43 event?

"Was there something wrong with that batch?" she asked Sam.

A dark shadow passed across Sam's face, and he looked suddenly older without his customary smile. He replaced the vase, hiding his exposed emotion.

"I just don't remember. It was over two years ago." Sam's face was swept clean by the time he stood back up. Sam was lying—she could tell. What had he remembered at that moment about kiln 43?

Molly pointed to a humdrum brown vase that looked identical to the two in George-Bradley's collection.

"Are those from later kilns?" she asked, amazed that the potter who had created such stunning work could suddenly produce something so bland.

"Yes. That's all he's made in the last two years. Brown vases. He gives them to C. C. to sell, but mostly a chain of florists from Winston-Salem buys them up. He doesn't sell to the public himself anymore. He's gone back to being a welder. Now," Sam said, obviously wanting to change the subject, "I've got some old Jugtown pieces on the bottom shelf, did you see those?"

Molly decided to press Sam just once more. "I would love to interview Jack. I want to see how he gets his forms so symmetrical," she said, trying to sound innocent.

Sam turned his gentle, frank face to her. "I don't think he'll talk to you."

Molly was surprised to hear this. "Why not?"

"He just doesn't do interviews anymore."

"Oh." Molly wished Sam would offer more information, but he was moving toward the door. Not wanting to push her friend any further, Molly reminded Sam that her jug was incomplete.

Sam perked up and said, "Let's make that face."

Molly found she had some skill at creating the face parts. Using a knife, she cut ears, a nose, brows, and lips from a slice of clay. Sam showed her how to score, but he seemed distracted, his eyes wandering over to the edge of the wood. Memories were swarming around him like bees. She could practically hear them buzzing.

Molly applied two horns and poked shallow eyeholes using a pencil. Then Sam showed her how to cut pieces of broken dishes for the teeth. She made them especially jagged and pointy, to complement the devil's fierce scowl.

"When you're in town next, you can pick him up. What color do you want to glaze him?"

"Really?" Molly couldn't hide her pleasure. She decided to give the jug to Mark once it was fired. "A nice, deep blue. I'm going to give him to a coworker. He's a Duke Blue Devils fan."

"Oh dear." Sam shook his head in mock sorrow. "There's only one basketball team in this state, and I believe they're called the UNC Tarheels."

Molly swept her arm around the building and said, "Well, I see some devils here, but I don't see a single ram."

"I'll get right to work on that." Sam laughed heartily.

Molly cleaned herself off again and got ready to go. She thanked Sam for his time and for introducing her to the wheel.

"You oughta give it a shot. Takes some time to get used to, but it's hard to stop once you start."

Molly shook her head. "I like it, I just don't think I'd be any good."

"It's in you, I can tell," Sam said seriously.

Molly glowed. "I think I will look into it. Thanks, Sam."

He walked her to her car, hands in overall pockets.

"Molly," Sam said as he opened her car door, "Jack Graham won't give interviews because he and his wife had some real trouble a couple of years ago. It's changed him.

He's not the same man he used to be. I'm just telling you so you don't go callin' him."

Molly couldn't tell whether he was worried for her sake or for Jack's.

"OK, I won't," she promised.

He seemed relieved. Backing down the driveway, she waved at the small, sweet man in mud-stained overalls.

Back on the main road, Molly's brain was spinning. Something happened with kiln number 43, but what? Was it something that would make a good article?

Sam's phrase followed after her like a cloud of dust: *They had some real trouble. It's changed him.*

Trouble.

The word rumbled through her air conditioner and over-powered the music from the radio. It sat in the stifling air under the black leather seats and fogged up the windows with its heat. Molly rolled down the windows to let it out, but it refused to budge.

Chapter 9

Inspired by her trip to Sam's, Molly headed for the closest megasized bookstore to learn more about the background of pottery making. Armed with a stack of heavy books and a cinnamon latte, Molly passed the afternoon lazily as she read up on wheel techniques, kiln building, and glaze recipes.

As Molly sat drinking her second cup of overpriced coffee, two young women sat down next to her and began poring hungrily over bridal magazines. One of them had apparently just gotten engaged and the other was her future maid of honor. Molly was distracted by their cries of "Look at this one!" as they ogled expensive dresses or squealed over the leg-of-mutton sleeves on some awful, fuchsia bridesmaid dress.

Soon, the floor space between their two tables was littered with a pile of books and magazines opened to glossy pages of glowing brides, flower-rimmed wedding cakes, and glittering engagement rings the size of small icebergs. Molly glanced down at one of the magazine covers featuring an article called "Fashion for Older Brides: Ages 30–40."

She frowned. "Older" was age thirty! She would already be considered an older bride. Ridiculous. Molly sighed, thinking of her mother's persistent nagging fear of Molly becoming a spinster. She didn't want to be a spinster either, but she certainly wasn't going to settle for Mr. So-So just to become a Mrs. So-So.

The former gloom of the day settled back on her shoulders like a cloak. First, there was Sam's warning to stay away from Jack Graham. Now, in a haven of books and caffeine that usually formed a comforting setting, Molly felt out of place. The pile of bridal magazines pointedly reminded her of her single status, and the magnificent sparkle of her neighbor's ring caught her eye with each excited wave of the girl's manicured hand. Every table in the café seemed to be occupied by chatting couples or smug women with wedding bands. Molly sighed. It was time to go.

Perhaps a connection with Mark was in order. If she could just get him out of the office again, they might have a chance to get to know one another better. Molly envisioned a candlelit table with Mark listening raptly to her witty conversation. Yes! She could take charge and ask *him* out. Molly had never asked a man out before, and she was terrified, but why not give it a shot? After all, it was a new century; roles were being redefined all the time.

Driving back to the office, she pictured Mark's laughing blue eyes and his easy smile. She thought about his calmness and the way he listened so attentively to everything she said. Fueled by determination, she checked her flawless complexion in the lobby mirrors, ran her fingers through her dark hair, and made her way to her desk with brisk, confident strides.

She decided to quickly check her voice mail before sailing off into the evening's sunset with Mark. She only had one message, and it was from Susan Black.

"Miss Appleby?" Susan's cool voice hummed through the receiver. "I received your message about doing an interview on my collection. Of course"—she made an effort to sound less frosty—"I would love to oblige, but I'd like to wait until *after* the Lex Lewis auction this weekend. You see, I plan to enhance my collection by adding *several* notable pieces from that sale. So let's plan on the week after, OK? *I'll* get in touch with *you* as to *when* I'll be available."

"Yes, Your Highness," Molly smirked, replacing the receiver. Then she made her way to Mark's office. Rapping lightly on his closed door, her insides churning, Molly could hear the sound of giggling coming from inside. Mark was not alone.

Suddenly, footsteps moved toward the door. Molly beat a hasty retreat to the nearest cover: a large fichus tree next to the water cooler. Peering between the leaves, Molly prayed that her green shirt would provide enough camouflage to avoid being spotted by Mark and his visitor.

Still giggling, a young, long-legged blonde stepped out of Mark's office with a smile on her full lips. She wore a pewter blouse in shimmering silk tucked into a short, brown suede skirt. High heels that came to a sharp point at the toe accentuated her trim legs. Her figure was all length and sinew. She was like a beautiful, blonde lioness. Swinging her long mane flirtatiously over one shoulder, she turned back to Mark and laid a graceful hand on his shoulder.

"You and I make such a great team," she purred.

Mark's cheeks reddened as he agreed. "I'm glad you had a chance to stop in today."

"Me too!" Blondie oozed, leaning into Mark's chest a little.

"Well . . ." Mark stammered, looking exactly as he had when Molly suggested they eat dinner together the other night. What a fool she had been! Did he perform his Mr. Shy routine on all women?

"Well nothing, darling." Blondie gave him a playful poke in the chest. "I'll see *you* tonight. Bye for now." She turned and sashayed down the hallway.

Mark stood rooted to the floor, watching the sultry figure sway away. Molly caught a whiff of a strong, musky perfume. Who was that woman? Was Mark dating someone after all? From the way they had talked together, they obviously weren't strangers. Molly felt crushed. She could never hope to compete with someone who had the body of a Barbie doll and the fashion sense of Audrey Hepburn. Even the woman's heady perfume created a glamorous signature in the air around her.

Feeling she was going to be sick from the overwhelming scent and her own humiliation, Molly waited until Mark went back inside his office, closing the door behind him. Then she moved out from her hiding place, took a deep drink from the tepid water cooler, and fled.

Chapter 10

The kiln is a constantly changing personality, from the lazy quiet beginning to the dramatic climax of full fire, flame issuing from all ports, and greedy demands for fuel.

—HARRY MEMMOTT, FROM *DISCOVERING POTTERY*

 olly woke the next morning hoping that the sultry figure she had seen yesterday had belonged to a dream. Surely, that long-legged sex goddess wasn't Mark's girlfriend. Walking blearily into the bathroom, Molly turned on the shower and took a hesitant look in the steamy mirror. She examined her curvy, big-boned body and compared herself to the thin, lithe blonde. She felt totally depressed.

"Apples and oranges," she muttered to her foggy reflection. "No, not even. More like celery and pears."

Molly dressed in loose, comfortable clothes, stuck her hair in a ponytail, and went downstairs to eat breakfast. The kitchen was strategically bare of comfort food, so she absently chewed on some nutritious cereal that was strongly reminiscent of the mulch she had recently put down around her bed of daylilies. Her sweltering car and an accident blocking both lanes leading to the office did nothing to improve her sour mood.

At work she sat listlessly at her desk and avoided looking in Mark's direction. It didn't take much of a sleuth to see how dejected she was, and when Clayton sat down opposite her later in the break room, he wasted no time in bringing up Mark.

"I can tell you saw our boy with that vixen yesterday," Clayton began, grimacing as he struggled with the wrapper of a banana MoonPie. "Did you smell that perfume? Ugh! Eau Du Tramp."

Molly smiled despite herself. "It was awfully musky, but she's still a stunning woman."

"Sure, if you like giggling twigs who smell like the cosmetic counter at JCPenny," Clayton said, closing his fingers over his nostrils as if the scent was still present.

"Do you think she's Mark's girlfriend?"

"I didn't think he had one and I know *everything* about *everyone's* love life." Clayton paused to think, his forefinger tugging at his bottom lip. "I can find out."

"How?" Molly asked cautiously.

Clayton took a dainty bite out of his MoonPie and dusted a smattering of crumbs from his shirt as if each one were a poisonous insect. "He's got an appointment book. If she was his girlfriend he won't have her written in. Heaven forbid if she is! I will have totally misjudged the man for having good taste. Or," he taunted, "I could just ask him."

"No!" Molly started. "Don't do that. He'll guess I put you up to it."

"Honey, you just leave it all to little ole Clayton. I'm not the Queen Bee around here for nothin'. Go get yourself busy with something and I'll be in touch." Clayton winked and touched his finger to his lips as he walked out of the room.

As she was ahead of schedule at work, Molly decided to spend the rest of the day at home in her sweatpants, napping with her cats. Swanson was out, no doubt enjoying the fine weather by playing eighteen holes of golf, so there was no one to question her absence.

Her late afternoon nap on the deck surrounded by birdsong and perky geraniums in terra-cotta pots was interrupted by a call from her mother. "Why aren't you at Lex's Preview Party?" she demanded.

Molly plucked a red gummy bear from its bag underneath her plastic chaise and dropped it into her mouth. "Well," she said, chewing, "I'll see all those people tomorrow."

"But you always go when you're covering an auction. And we managed to work in a dozen of George-Bradley's best pieces into tomorrow's sale by making an addendum to the catalogue. It's mobbed here already. So why aren't you coming?"

Molly hesitated. She was upset about the discovery of Mark's date and possible girlfriend, but she also didn't feel like getting dressed up in order to talk shop. She felt like an evening of TV, her two cats, and a good sulk.

"I'm just tired," Molly told her mother.

"Fine. Listen, there's another reason I'm calling. I heard something on the radio today about Hillary Keane. Apparently he's been *found,* whatever that means. I couldn't hear anything else because Lex was on the cell phone gushing nauseating sweet nothings to Kitty. There's going to be something about it on the six o'clock news. I thought you'd be interested."

"He's been found?" Molly wondered, the candy on her

palm forgotten. "As in his *body* or as in discovered holed up in some seedy motel room with two kilos of coke?"

"I don't know. In between all the sickening 'cinnabuns' and 'sugar plums' all I heard was Hillary's name and full details at six. You'd better watch," Clara said.

"Wow! Listen, I have to tell you what I discovered about him when I stopped by the pharmacy." Molly quickly filled Clara in on her visit with Brandy. "I am going to be glued to that TV tonight, aren't you?"

"No. I came over to the gallery early to give the boys some directions for tomorrow. I'm running the floor and that means it's my responsibility to make sure they hold up the one-drawer stand instead of the umbrella stand tomorrow. Lex couldn't find people who knew less about antiques if he picked them blindfolded."

Molly laughed, imagining her mother henpecking the four young men hired to lift furniture during sales. True, they weren't the sharpest tools in the shed, but at least they were capable of carrying huge wardrobes and heavy chests of drawers to people's cars. Those old pieces of furniture were solid masses of wood, awkward to carry and even harder to cram into the spaces of minivans and SUVs.

"That makes it all more exciting," she teased her mother, feeling revived by the news about Keane. "Plus, you are a natural at bossing people around."

"Hmph," Clara snorted. "Anymore excitement and I'll be starting my cocktail hour right after lunch. 'Night dear."

Molly stretched out on the couch and leafed through an antiques magazine while she waited for the news to come on. She mulled over her motives for not attending the preview. Normally, she lined up a future interview during this time—someone she was sure would spend a lot of money at the auction the following day. Now, she would have to cover the auction and acquire an interview candidate at the same time.

She admitted to herself that another reason for avoiding the party was that she hoped for a phone call from Clayton.

Popping several more candies in her mouth, she switched to the local news. The leadoff story concerned a national kidnapping case that, for once, had resulted in a happy ending. The little girl who had been taken to an abandoned house and tied to a pipe with duct tape had chewed through the tape and shouted for help from a broken window. The footage showed her safely at home with her parents and grandmother, being hugged tightly and given flowers and plush animals from the neighbors.

Molly was pleasantly surprised to see a positive story leading off the nightly news. She never watched it anymore because the focus was either on a grisly crime or political scandal. After a teaser about a possible baseball strike and a long commercial break, the anchorwoman lifted her shiny crown of platinum blonde hair and announced the capture of an antiquities thief in the western part of the state.

"This afternoon in Hendersonville," she intoned in a voice of dried up honey, "authorities arrested forty-four-year-old Hillary Keane on charges of theft and driving under the influence. Sources say Keane swerved off the road, nearly hitting a jogger, before colliding with the guardrail and coming to a stop. Here's Phil with more."

The screen switched to a mountain road winding its way through a small town. The reporter, frowning in well-rehearsed consternation, stood before a curve in the road where the guardrail had buckled beneath the weight of Keane's van. The van was being removed on a flatbed tow truck behind Phil as he gave his report:

"This is the scene of what could have been a serious tragedy. Hillary Keane, a pharmacist from Asheboro, was swerving all over this twisted stretch of road when he almost hit Hendersonville's Clyde Farmer. Farmer was out jogging, hoping to get in a midday run before heading back to work at the post office. He almost didn't make it. When he saw Keane's oncoming vehicle, Farmer leapt over the guardrail in an attempt to avoid the oncoming car. He missed being hit by a matter of seconds. Farmer suffered minor injuries from his fall and is being treated at the local hospital."

Phil gestured at the guardrail and continued, "As if driving under the influence weren't enough, Keane is in even more hot water. Authorities report that several bins of stolen pottery were found in his battered vehicle. The pieces belong to different collectors across the state and are thought to be extremely valuable. Keane admitted that he was planning to sell them to an unknown buyer from Pennsylvania. Fortunately, none of the valuables were damaged in the crash. Authorities are *now* trying to discover who *else* was involved in the resale of the stolen goods. Keane is currently being held without bail. This is his second offense of driving while impaired." Phil produced a judgmental frown. "Marion, back to you."

"Hmm." Marion shook her shingled hair in disdain. "Looks like *someone* has a lot of explaining to do. Thanks, Phil. Up next, a Raleigh man gains much more than a pet when he visits his local animal shelter. Stay with us."

As the commercial break began, Molly frantically dialed the number to Lex's gallery. When Kitty answered, she asked her to fetch Clara to the phone right away.

"What's going on?" Kitty asked.

"Mom will tell you, just find her!"

When Clara heard the news, she was astounded. "A thief! I never would have guessed. I've seen him at sales for years. He seemed like a complete gentleman."

"I think he was to some people." Molly told Clara about the girl Keane had helped at the pharmacy. "Still, I bet Keane *was* stealing George-Bradley's pottery and he *was* found out. And now we know that he had a prior conviction for drunk driving. He probably had a hell of a time driving with those hands even when he was sober. Do you know what I'm thinking?"

"You still believe there's a connection to George-Bradley's death?"

"Maybe he just supplied the insulin. With such advanced rheumatoid arthritis, I don't think it's possible for him to have directly given George-Bradley the shot, but he's still a shady character."

Clara paused. "Keane was after pottery. He was greedy, but I don't see him aiding a killer. And why help someone kill George-Bradley now? Who else would benefit from his death?" Molly heard a crash in the background. "Listen, I can't think about all this detective stuff right now. I've still got so much to do here and Tweedledee and Tweedledum aren't getting any smarter."

Molly grinned. "I assume those are your new helpers. How's the crowd?"

"It's been super-busy. This should be a terrific sale. Lex is going to rake it in."

"Good for him. He works so hard for it."

"So do I!" Clara pretended to be hurt.

"And you do, too, Ma. See you in the morning."

Molly cooked chicken in a creamy mustard sauce for dinner and then watched the ten o'clock news to see if there were anymore updates on Keane. What had that man been thinking? Why was he so desperate to sell the pottery that he stole from other collectors? Did he only steal from people he disliked as a kind of revenge? Was he an accessory to murder as well as a thief and a drunk? Maybe the girl in the pharmacy was covering for him. She obviously cared for him deeply, so she'd gladly give him an alibi.

Turning down her bedsheet, Molly stroked Griffin's soft brown and black fur as he curled up next to her. If Keane was guilty of being an accessory, she was sure the police would follow the trail created by the stolen pottery.

Inevitably, that trail would lead them to George-Bradley's house, where they would learn about his friendship with Keane from Bunny. Next, they would link the day of George-Bradley's death with Keane's sudden exodus. They would interview people who knew both men, and someone, like Donald, would tell them about the night George-Bradley called his former friend a thief. Linking all these clues together, the police would realize this was not a case of accidental death. They would ferret out the truth about Keane and question him about the person he had helped murder a man no one seemed to miss.

Satisfied that the mysterious death of the infamous pottery collector was about to be solved by capable professionals, Molly drifted off to sleep.

Chapter 11

People need pots. You can see that from the way they love to look at them, to handle and to buy.

—ROSEMARY ZORZA, FROM *POTTERY: CREATING WITH CLAY*

A low fog hung out the window, holding the humidity hostage. Blades of grass reached wearily upward as dewdrops weighed down their yellow green ridges. It was early. Even the birds were silent. No cars passed by, lawn mowers rested in their sheds, and children were still turning in their sleep, dreaming of triple-decker ice cream cones and riding their bikes to the pool where they would find the courage to dive off the high board.

Molly's alarm pierced the tranquility with the high shrill of a Victorian policeman's whistle. Her cats remained immobile on the bed, their eyes closed in tight slits as they burrowed farther into their own feathery stomachs and ignored her movements as she shuffled downstairs to make coffee.

Once she reached Lex's gallery, she noticed that the parking lot was awfully full for an auction that didn't start for another two hours. Before the sale started, Molly typically photographed the items she believed would bring the highest prices, but today she could see this might prove difficult if mobs of people were trying to preview pieces before the sale.

Clara agreed it would obviously be a challenge. "I told you that you should have come last night." She met her daughter at the checkout counter. "How are you going to take pictures with all these people around?"

"I'll manage." Molly smiled at the signs of her mother's unusual nervousness, watching her scan over the catalogue. Molly knew that organized, capable Clara had the location of every item memorized and could run the sale in her sleep, but her mother still worried. "Some friendly use of good manners is all it'll take. Don't worry Ma, it's going to be a great sale."

Clara closed her catalogue and frowned. "I don't know," she said gloomily. "I woke up with this bad feeling that something was going to go wrong today."

Molly did not dismiss her mother's instinctual feelings—like her own, they had too often proved correct.

"Like what? Lex has obviously gotten enough interest. I looked at the Internet bids last night and many things have already reached their estimates and the sale hasn't even begun."

Clara lowered her voice. "It's not the prices. It's something else."

"You didn't say anything to Lex about your vibe, did you?" Molly asked.

"Of course not." Her mother gestured to where Lex stood chatting up one of his frequent buyers. "He's already got a fever."

"Not again!" Molly couldn't help grinning. Lex habitually ran fevers before one of his quarterly sales. These were the ones that brought in the real profits for him. His weekly sales just paid the rent, and since he and Kitty were dreaming of buying a new love nest, this sale was especially important.

Molly watched him pat his forehead with a tissue before moving on to refocus the projection screen. Lex also hired people to hold the smaller items aloft so the crowd could view them. After they were sold, the items were brought down to a holding area where they were later packed and given over to their new owners.

Between the Internet bidding and the live bids, Lex needed a large crew to run one of his premier sales, and though Molly enjoyed working the sales as much as Clara did, she found she could not glean the details she needed for her *Collector's Weekly* article while dashing to and fro looking for a snuffbox or a set of sterling spoons to hold up for the crowd.

Inside the main room, groups of buyers clustered before the display cases, carefully examining the selections of southern pottery, some of which were from George-Bradley's collection. A sign taped to the sliding glass doors read, Please do not handle the pottery. Ask for Assistance. It was being completely ignored as collectors and dealers held pieces out to the light, searching for minute cracks or flakes to the rims.

They swiveled jugs upside down, looking for the potter's stamp or a date. Each did their best to appear disinterested in the piece they examined, setting their faces into ambivalent masks as they ran their fervent fingers over the curves of clay. It was always the hands that gave their desire away.

Molly spotted Donald handling a pottery poodle glazed in earth brown. She watched Donald's face as he angled

the piece and bobbed his head up and down so that his bi-
focal glasses could absorb all the details. Brows knit in
concentration; he replaced the handsome poodle in its case
and made a note in his sale catalogue. He liked the piece.

"You planning on buying up the whole showcase?"
Molly greeted him with a teasing pat on the arm.

"Hello!" Donald hugged her warmly. "I might not be
able to afford the prices today, but that N. Fox jug in the
third case is a keeper." He glanced worriedly at the stream
of incoming buyers, more of whom were filtering wide-
eyed into the room like fish released into the open sea.

"Looks like a lot of people waited to preview until today," Molly said, following his gaze.

"It sure does," Donald agreed. "I came on Monday night
so I could take a long look in private. It's good to have a
friend *inside*," Donald nodded in acquiescence in Clara's
direction, "but I still like to get here early and get my seat."

Molly looked over at the end of the first row and saw
Donald's name taped to a chair.

"I'd better shoot some of these pieces before they get
mobbed again." She excused herself and got to work taking photographs of the items she expected to fetch the
highest prices.

It was almost impossible to interview bidders before a
sale. They were too preoccupied and reluctant to say anything that could indicate their preferences. Molly focused
on taking all the photos she could, then ambled over to the
front desk where Kitty was registering bidders and handing out reserved seating cards.

"Hey Kitty." Molly greeted her friend with a quick hug.
"Is it going to be a full house?"

"And then some," her friend said as she patted the pile
of bidder numbers. They were already up over the hun-

dreds. "We had to rent extra chairs, and people will still be standing."

Lex came over in search of his absentee bid sheets, his eyes darting about without seeing. Kitty placed an arm on his chest and handed him a bottle of water and three aspirin.

"You burning hunk of man, take these and I'll get you the sheets. I know exactly where they are."

Lex kissed her cheek and downed the aspirin. Molly got some short quotes on his feelings about the prime pieces in the sale, but then he was hailed by several prospective buyers and had no more time for chatting.

"We've got a problem," Clara said gravely as she appeared from the back room, holding one of the cordless phones in her hand. "Wade just called. Craven threw his back out last night and neither of them is coming! What are we going to do?"

Wade and Craven were experienced auction workers. They could lift the heaviest pieces of furniture without breaking a sweat and courteously help customers load their goods at the end of each sale.

Molly looked at her watch. It was 9:30 and the auction was scheduled to begin in thirty minutes. Two of the four men had called out sick. The other two were new and would be scrambling to move and locate all of the furniture during the sale. Also, there was so much pottery to be displayed, taken to the back, and carefully wrapped without damage. It was a serious problem.

"I don't think Will and Matt can handle the whole job!" Kitty wailed dramatically in between chewing on her nails. "They are too green!"

"They don't have any choice!" Clara snapped. "Today is the day Will learns what a mantel is." And she hurried off to find her victims.

Just then, Will shuffled in and grabbed a soda off the patron's buffet table. Clara appeared with hands on hips, a clear sign that she was unhappy. "What kind of outfit is that for working?"

Will's cap covered his eyes completely, and he had to peek out from under its brim to read the listing. As he snaked away from Clara's glare in order to review the listing of furniture he was to move, Molly noticed an odd shadowing on his skin. Browns, greens, and blues swirled around his eyes like smudges of paint. The left side of his lower lip was bloated and hung slightly forward, and a small cut worked its way through his upper chin.

"What happened to you?" Molly asked in concern. She didn't really know Will or Matt well as they were relatively new crewmembers, but she was shocked into bluntness by the sight of his bruises.

"Got in a fight," Will mumbled, a gleam of pride in his sunken eyes.

"When? Last night?" Molly couldn't believe he had been out carousing the night before one of the big sales.

"Nah, Thursday," Will said nonchalantly and walked off.

"Looks like you lost!" a bent old lady who was a regular buyer called after him, cackling maliciously.

Finally, it was time for the auction to begin. The last stragglers took their seats while those who were too edgy to sit found places to stand behind the back rows. Lex came to the podium to make his opening announcements. Molly winked encouragingly at Clara as her mother surveyed the crowd, her crew poised to begin the frantic pace. From his elevated platform, Lex reminded the crowd that all of the items had been available to preview for over a week and that all purchases were final. Most of the audience talked through his opening speech, having heard it all a dozen times before.

"Lastly, thank you all for coming. Let's get started, shall we? Lot 1. We have a fine gentleman's shaving stand out of cherry. Excellent patina on this early piece. Let's start it off at $100. Now $150. Now $200. Thank you."

Just as the item closed at a selling price of $750 plus buyer's premium, the power went off. The lights winked out and the humming computers went silent. The projection screen turned black and the air-conditioning ceased flowing through the vents. The crowd sat agog for a fraction of a second, before turning about in their chairs and twittering animatedly with their neighbors.

Lex was frozen at the podium, but as he blinked his eyes and began to step down, the power snapped back on. He wiped his forehead in a dramatic gesture of relief and the crowd laughed.

"Can you reboot?" he called over to the two girls running the computers.

"Yeah, just give us a second."

While Lex entertained the crowd with a story about another auction disaster, the computers were brought back to life and the image of Lot 2, a painted humidor, leapt onto the projection screen. Molly looked at her mother, whose mouth was set in a thin line of concern. Was this the event she had had a premonition about?

Then, Matt, the other new crew member, pushed past Molly's seat in order to retrieve a cast-iron urn placed in a far corner. She recoiled at the strong smell of stale beer and cigarette smoke that hung in a tight cloud around his body. She also noticed that he bent to pick up a pottery jardinière instead of the iron urn.

"No, not that one," she whispered to him, pointing to the correct piece, "that one in the corner."

He turned to thank her, his eyes bloodshot and puffy

with fatigue. As she watched him reach out to grasp the urn, she saw that his hands were shaking. He was certainly not in a good state to be carrying valuable antiques. As he moved to grab the urn by its rim, she leaned over again, turning her nose away from his barroom odor.

"Grab it by the handles or the base. You'll drop it that way," she scolded. "And you'd better drink some water."

If Lex had any idea Matt was still inebriated on the day of his big sale, he would burst, but that reaction was nothing compared to the wrath Matt would face from Clara should he disturb the flow of the sale. With the veteran workers absent, Molly could see that the expectations set for Matt and Will were just too high. She was torn between sympathy and disgust for the irresponsible boys.

When Clara next came her way, loading her hands with two crystal decanters, Molly warned her of potential disasters.

"Matt's got a nasty hangover," she whispered.

"Hangover? The boy is dead drunk!" Clara retorted and whisked her items up to the front.

Twenty lots later, Matt was nowhere in sight.

"Molly." Kitty appeared at her side, gripping her arm like a vise. "Matt left. He just left!"

"What?" Molly asked, astounded.

Kitty whispered urgently, "He left! He said he was peeing blood and had to go to the hospital."

Molly looked across the room at her mother, who was scrambling to prepare a table full of pottery to be auctioned off in the next few minutes. "Oh Lord."

"You've got to get up there! Your mom can't handle all this," Kitty pleaded.

Molly left her notepad on her chair and wove her way around the standing observers until she reached the front.

She whispered the dire news to Clara, who unhesitatingly shoved a catalogue in her hands.

"I *told* you something bad was going to happen. Still, I'd rather have you up here anyway. You're now in charge of all the pottery. I'll grab you if we need to lift something small. Otherwise, we're going to have to use the wand."

The wand was a stick with a star glued to its tip that the crew used to point to objects that were just too bulky to bring up front for the crowd to view.

"We have the projection screen, too," Molly reminded her mother. "They'll know what we're selling." And she quickly grabbed the next lot, a pottery lamb, and held it aloft before the audience.

Lex did a double take when he saw her, but didn't miss a beat of his selling lilt. As he opened the bidding, Molly watched the same old lady who had cackled at Will hold her bidder number firmly in the air. Donald raised his as well, and it came down to just the two of them fighting for the pottery animal. Finally, Donald shook his head and looked back down at his lap, a sign that he was done bidding. The old woman lifted her face and smiled with pleasure.

"That lady is having a ball," Molly whispered.

"I'm glad *someone* is," Clara returned, waving for Will to pick up the next lot.

As Molly watched him carry a Persian runner up to the front, her eyes fell on a familiar puff of hair in the audience.

Bunny Staunton was seated in the third row. She had never come to one of Lex's sales before, but since some of her late husband's pottery was about to be sold, she probably wanted to bear witness to its true value. Catching Molly's eye, she gave a cursory nod of recognition, then turned her gaze to the next lot, the first of her husband's collection.

The piece, a Ben Owen two-handled tapered vase glazed in Chinese blue with large patches of red, was an extremely handsome item. The large amount of red glaze seeping through like a sunrise would raise the price, and bidding cards flapped around the room like white wings, eager to be spotted.

Finally, the last two bidders battled it out. One was a man seated toward the back wearing jeans and a faded flannel shirt. Molly knew, despite his casual dress, that he was quite wealthy and was a fervent pottery collector as well. She craned her neck to catch a view of the second bidder and instantly recognized the neat, trim figure wearing a silk blouse and a double strand of pearls. It was Susan, George-Bradley's former mistress.

She sat on the opposite side of the room from Bunny, about two rows back. She could observe Mrs. Staunton, but Bunny couldn't see her. Susan's lips, shiny with a trendy gloss, were pursed in dogged determination as she won the lot. She made a notation in her catalogue and prepared to bid on the next. As each piece of George-Bradley's collection came up for sale, she waged a relentless war against other bidders until she laid claim to the majority of his better pieces.

Soon, several people turned to see who the persistent buyer was, including a disgruntled Donald. Even Bunny was curious, and she turned to look behind her shoulder just as a large C. C. Burle devil face jug came up for sale. It was the very piece Susan and George-Bradley had wrestled over at the kiln opening. Susan sat erect in her chair, raising her bidding card with delicate flicks of her tiny wrist.

From her vantage point, Molly could see the two women clearly. As she held up an unsigned whiskey jug for the audience to view, she watched Bunny discover who the bidder was. Susan glanced over at Bunny, her bidding card held up like a shield.

The two women locked eyes, but only for a moment, exchanging looks of venomous loathing before Bunny sneered in disdain and turned back around. Molly could see that underneath her thick makeup and attempts to control her expression, Bunny's eyes were filled with a cold rage. She looked down at her catalogue, cheeks flushed with anger and humiliation.

"Poor Bunny," Molly whispered to Clara, as mother and daughter witnessed the other woman's misery.

Clara, who never missed a single detail of the entire sale, handed Molly an antique Cherokee basket. "This is next. I know, I feel bad for her too."

For Bunny, this should have been a moment of triumph. Like the photographs in her home, Bunny had appeared at the sale as the devoted wife of the late George-Bradley Staunton. Everyone attending the auction knew who she was and had paid respect to her husband and to his collection. If his pottery sold well, it only increased her husband's reputation as a collector and made it easier to maintain her illusion of having married a well-known man with impeccable taste. The presence of her husband's former mistress evaporated that image into mist.

As the last of George-Bradley's pottery sold, Bunny made her way to the restroom. When she returned, she passed right by the row where her reserved seat was and crossed into the front room. Through the window, Molly saw her open the door to her silver BMW and sit down inside without starting the ignition.

Unable to pay any more attention to Bunny, Molly and Clara worked like frenzied bees for the next two hours. In between lots, they guzzled water and took hasty bites of salami and cheese sandwiches. By the last lot, they were dead on their feet.

As buyers lined up to pay Kitty for their items Lex asked, "Can one of you guys help wrap some pottery?" He was still ignorant of what the three of them had accomplished without Matt's help.

"No," Clara said wearily. "The customers can wrap their own. We've had it."

"Where's Matt?" Lex looked around.

Clara filled Lex in on the details of Matt's departure as Molly moved her leaden legs down to the wrapping area to assist with the pottery. Of course it was Susan's huge pile that required so much attention, but Lex was almost out of boxes.

"Do you have anything to pack these in?" she asked Susan with as much politeness as she could muster.

"I *might* have some bins in my car," she replied haughtily. "But I would expect *you* to provide boxes since I'm spending all this money."

"I'll come out with you to fetch them," Molly offered reluctantly, her fatigue and dislike for the petite woman causing her to wish she had not volunteered to help. She wondered if Susan would be embarrassed about being so snotty when Molly showed up on her doorstep a few days later for their interview. Right now, Susan thought Molly was simply another member of Lex's crew, unworthy of cordiality.

"Oh fine, let's go," Susan drawled. "But hurry up, I don't have all day."

Susan's white Mercedes SUV looked brand new. Molly wondered what Susan did for a living to be able to afford such an expensive car and lot after lot of costly pottery. Her car retailed for around $70,000, and she had probably spent $10,000 at today's sale. All of her clothes were designer labels and her shoes alone were the latest fashion of monogrammed leather that cost $300 a pair.

As Molly climbed into Susan's car to dig out plastic bins, Bunny suddenly appeared at Susan's side. Inside the car, Molly pivoted her body to watch as Bunny raised her hand and pointed a shiny, manicured talon at Susan's chest.

"How dare you!" Bunny breathed heavily. "How dare you show up here and bid on *my* husband's things!"

Susan was completely unruffled. She looked Bunny up and down in disgust and shook her coiffed crown of hair. "Last time I checked, this was a *public* auction."

"You piece of trash. I know where you came from. People like you never shake off the trailer park dirt, no matter what you drive or wear." Bunny waved at Susan's clothes in dismissal.

Through the open car door, Molly could see the heat rise in Susan's face. The "trailer park" comment had hit home.

"You husband didn't seem to mind," Susan retorted in a low, taunting voice. Then she ran her hands over her small hips and smiled evilly.

Bunny looked as if an arrow struck her. Molly was afraid that the malicious look on Bunny's face meant she was about to do something rash. Instead, she simply hissed, "You were just another *thing* he collected!"

Turning away, Bunny seemed to think of one more verbal dagger she could thrust into Susan. "By the way," she said, turning back to Susan and grinning slyly, "My lawyer paid me a visit this week. You know, to review *my* husband's estate. He gave me a sealed letter that George-Bradley had left for me to read in the event he should die before me. I found it *most* interesting. Do you want to know what it said?"

Susan stood silently, her face empty of expression. She looked as though she had forgotten how to breathe.

And then, leaning in as if she were going to kiss Susan on the cheek, Bunny began whispering something into her ear. Molly brazenly scooted over the warm surface of Susan's leather seat in order to get closer to the open door, but the only thing she was able to catch was "your little car ride in the backwoods that day."

Susan's face, which had been screwed up in anger, rapidly blanched chalk white and her eyes grew round in shock. She stood rooted to the ground, fists clenched at her sides like a hoplite statue. All the fight was gone from her. Triumphant, Bunny walked away, slowly and with careful dignity. Molly saw her opportunity to leave, grabbed her bins as quietly as possible, and scurried back to the gallery.

As she watched Susan drive off with all her pottery left behind, Clara came to stand beside her.

"Susan left without her pottery!" Clara exclaimed. Sinking down into the nearest chair, she mused tiredly, "Who won *that* fight, I wonder."

Molly thought about the circumstances that tied the opposing women together. Bunny was now a widow, desperately trying to hold on to her public image as George-Bradley's happy wife. Susan, whose passion for pottery had once united her with the same man, now sought to buy all the pieces George-Bradley had owned.

Somehow, Susan's relationship with George-Bradley had soured. They had become rivals, fighting over pottery at C. C.'s kiln opening like two children squabbling over a toy in the playground.

What had Bunny whispered about a "car ride" to elicit such a powerful reaction? It must have meant something awful to Susan to make her leave behind thousands of dollars of pottery, even temporarily.

Molly sighed, thinking about her first impression of George-Bradley. He had been rude, lecherous, and greedy. Why would any woman fight over a man like him?

She shrugged. "No one won, Ma. In fact, I think we just witnessed Round One."

Chapter 12

Pottery making is a discipline that, once one is thoroughly hooked, is like an addiction and almost impossible to separate from.

—ROBIN HOPPER, FROM *FUNCTIONAL POTTERY FORM AND AESTHETIC IN POTS OF PURPOSE*

Late that afternoon, Molly reviewed the note cards scattered in an arc across her work desk. After quickly forming the outline to her next article, she planned to go home and take a well-deserved nap out on her cozy deck.

"Hello, love." Clayton stood before her wearing a pink and blue striped shirt and designer jeans with cowboy boots.

"You always look so good, Clayton."

"Honey, you look like last week's wash. Look at your nails. You have been *terribly* negligent of those cuticles," Clayton admonished her.

"Doesn't anyone take a day off around here?" Molly asked testily.

"Temper, temper. Clayton here just came to share with you some news about that Keane fellow. See, I was on the phone with darling Francis over at the *Sun Times* and oh, that boy has a body like—"

"Clayton! Don't be a tease," Molly interrupted him.

Clayton sulked. He liked to build up his story before getting to the good gossip.

"Oh all right, I'm sorry. Tell me about Keane now and then you can give me every detail about Francis and his physique over a cappuccino after work. My treat," added Molly.

Clayton relented. "Yummy. Oh, I can't resist those eyelashes of yours. It's a deal. Well, seems that Keane got his liquor on pretty early the day he almost hit that jogger. Started out at a truck stop where he was giving a little lift to his coffee out of a flask and later ended up drinking beer at some pool hall that calls itself a restaurant. Heading back to his seedy motel, where he's been holed up for the last week, he almost hit that jogger," Clayton stuck out his tongue in distaste. "I mean, Sweet Jesus, who stays in a motel anymore?"

"Was this seedy motel in Asheboro?"

Clayton paused to think. "No. Just outside Hendersonville. The waitresses at the truck stop all remembered him because he came in every morning to drink coffee laced with bourbon. Thing is, the little dear could never get the cap back on his bourbon flask. Bad case of the shakes, I guess."

"Not exactly. He was acting like a guilty man who happens to be afflicted with rheumatoid arthritis. He may have stolen pottery, but now I know he couldn't have killed George-Bradley. I wonder how he could drive at all with those hands."

Molly was done thinking about Keane. Clara was right. Keane was interested in pottery, not murder. It had to have been Bunny or Susan who had given George-Bradley the extra dose of insulin.

Her thoughts turned back to the scene from the auction. Bunny's whisper and Susan's shocked face. What else had George-Bradley written in that letter? And that calm rage was certainly a side of Bunny that Molly hadn't guessed the older woman possessed. Bunny must have done the murder! She was alone in the house with her husband and was the only other person who had access to his medicine. Of course, she had wanted revenge. But why now? She needed to get into Bunny's house and find out more about George-Bradley's widow. It was time to arrange an interview with Mrs. Staunton.

"Miss Molly," Clayton interrupted her thoughts, "I do believe you haven't listened to a word I was saying. Let's go get that manicure. I can tell you need a break."

"You're right, let me just check my messages first. I forgot to listen to them yesterday."

There was only one new voice mail message. As Molly listened, a muffled voice began speaking. A cold, menacing tone crept through the receiver. "Stay out of things that don't concern you," the voice threatened slowly. "Some stones are better left unturned. If you don't, you'll be sorry. Watch your back, you stupid girl." The message ended.

"Molly? Honey?" She heard Clayton's voice as if from a long way off.

She handed him the phone and replayed the message.

"Sweet Jesus and the Saints!" Clayton cried, dropping the phone as if it were on fire. His hands fluttered in the air like startled birds as he shrieked, "We've got to call the police!"

Clayton dialed and released a loud and frantic tirade to the unfortunate soul who answered the phone.

Wanting to avoid listening to the message again, Molly walked numbly to the ladies' room where she splashed cold water on her face and tried to digest the threatening message. It had not sounded familiar; the voice was too muffled to be distinctive. She couldn't even tell if it had been a man or a woman. It had been recorded last night, but that meant nothing. She needed to sit down and think this through.

Who had she talked to about her theories? Only to people she knew well. So who had called her? Bunny? She had no idea Molly suspected her of murder. Susan? Could Susan have killed George-Bradley, and Bunny had discovered proof within the letter? Was that the whole secret Bunny had whispered in Susan's ear today?

Still, none of these theories explained why Molly would have received the call last night. Clayton suddenly interrupted her thoughts in his full dramatic glory. He flung open the restroom door with a cry and dragged her into the break room. Clucking like a mother hen, he plied Molly with coffee and a stale cheese Danish and wrung his hands over her until a policeman arrived.

Molly issued a brief statement, and though Clayton did his best to elevate the seriousness of the matter, the policeman didn't seem overwhelmingly concerned.

"Press people get death threats all the time," he said flatly, removing one of Clayton's hands from his arm. "Usually not at papers like this, but it happens. Just let me know if it happens again." He turned to Molly, giving her his card.

"Thanks," she mumbled, grateful she had not shared any of her theories about the murder. The policeman would certainly assume she was reading too many mysteries and in desperate need of male attention.

Clayton followed him out, gushing about the shock it had caused him. Molly heard a third voice enter the conversation as she stacked her index cards and packed her bag to go home. It was Mark's soft tenor coming from the lobby.

"Are you OK?" he said, appearing at her side moments later.

Thinking back to his leggy blonde visitor, she replied without looking at him. "Yes, I'm fine."

As she picked up her bag and moved to leave, Mark blocked her path. Startled, she looked up at him.

"Clayton told me what happened. He's a wreck, but I'm worried about *you*. Can't I do something?" he asked.

"No." Her voice softened. Mark really was a nice guy, even if he had a girlfriend. "Thank you, though."

"I don't think you should be alone tonight. Do you feel up to going out for dinner?"

"Can't. I already promised my mother I'd come over. Also," Molly paused, looking at Mark shrewdly, "I'd like to go out to dinner with you, but I'm not sure that blonde I saw you with the other day would approve."

Mark looked confused, then laughed in relief. "Amy? Amy Byrd? That was a business meeting. Amy's a rep for Grant's Auction House over in Wilson. They are going to start running large, weekly ads with the paper. She's not my girlfriend."

"Oh." Molly was embarrassed. "It's just that I heard her saying she'd see you later that night and I assumed . . ."

"That was some party for one of my med school friends. She's dating an old buddy of mine. I wish she wasn't dating him, though. She's an awful flirt. Plus," he smiled down at her, "I don't go in for stick figures."

"What a nice thing to say, Mark Harrison." Molly was pleased. She forgot all about the intimidating message as she gazed up into his twinkling blue eyes. "What *is* your type then?" She astonished herself by asking.

Mark opened his mouth and spoke as many words in one breath as she had heard him say in the two years they had worked for the same paper. "I like a woman with smarts. Someone with a good heart and a quick laugh. I like a woman to look like a woman. Someone who will eat dinner with you instead of pushing two pieces of lettuce around on her plate, as she looks around to see who might be admiring her. I like a woman who believes in family, friends, and the American flag. A woman who has framed photos of her cats on her desk." Mark exhaled. He looked as surprised as Molly by the length of his monologue. "I like a woman like you. You're my type," he finished with a soft whisper and then leaned in to kiss her.

Chapter 13

Despite the falling rain and crackling of the flames, everyone heard the detonations . . . Generally it is the larger, thicker-walled wares that suffer the most; the smaller pots in the case showed no damage at all.

—CHARLES G. ZUG III, FROM *TURNERS AND BURNERS*

Monday morning dawned at the Staunton Estate without its usual birdsong and squirrel chatter. Instead, a row of pickups and workmen in jeans broke the stillness with the sharp staccato of hammering, the whine of hand-held saws, and the crackling of snapping wood.

Two men in jeans and black T-shirts carried the massive shelves that once held George-Bradley's pottery collection outside. Handmade from solid walnut, they were both heavy and attractive, but Bunny told the foreman he could keep the whole lot.

"What's Walt gonna do with these?" one worker asked another.

"Use 'em," grunted the second beneath the weight of the shelves, "for books."

"Books?" The first man laughed as they slid the shelves onto the bed of one of the trucks.

"He's a Civil War buff, remember?"

The two men headed back inside. The oriental rugs in the main hall had been removed and sheets of plastic covered the hardwood floors. A thin layer of dust had already settled upon the sheet, and the buzz of power tools grew louder inside the wing where George-Bradley had once spent most of his free time.

Inside the music room, two men were ripping up the dark brown carpet and rolling it in wide strips to be hauled outside. In the office, the last of the shelves was being removed while two men stood over the massive mahogany desk and admired its waxy surface. The drawers were still stuffed with stationary, rubber bands, staples, and sundry supplies.

"Hey Chief!" one of the men called out.

A tall man wearing a short-sleeved, plaid button-down stepped inside. He removed his John Deere baseball cap, wiped the sweat from his brow, and surveyed the room.

"What've you boys got?"

"What's the plan for this desk?"

The foreman, Walter Hogue, ran his calloused hand over the leather and wood desktop. He understood, without being knowledgeable about antiques, that the piece had been made by hand. The workmanship was so fine that he had trouble finding the joinery.

"Hidden dovetails." He nodded in admiration. He stood and gestured outside. "Unfortunately, it goes out to the garage for now. The lady doesn't want anything left in here."

"Just clear the whole place out, is that the plan?" one of the men asked.

"Yep. Seems the lady's sister is moving in and this is going to be her part of the house."

"Shoot, there's enough room upstairs to house the

whole choir of Shady Grove Baptist, why go through all this renovation?"

Walt shrugged his wide, bony shoulders. "Don't know. Everyone needs their own space, I guess."

"Well, it's her money." The two men strained under the weight of the desk and Walt jumped in to lend a hand.

Passing the library, he noticed the rest of his crew standing in a group before the wall facing the window.

"Y'all studying something?" he called out.

One of the workers pointed at the fine mahogany wall paneling with his sledgehammer. "Chief, are we really supposed to tear all this out?"

Another man lifted his crowbar. "It seems crazy to dig into this stuff. It must of cost a fortune. Are you sure she wants it all bashed?"

Walt gazed around the room again. He had gone over every detail with Mrs. Staunton, making sure that he had gotten all of her instructions precisely. It wouldn't do to make a mistake when it came to such fine paneling. He had asked her the same question. It was such excellent workmanship, was she sure she wanted it removed? She was positive. She had even handed him a can of paint called perky periwinkle to use on the new walls.

"Look boys, the lady said it made the room too dark and too masculine for her sister, so she wants it out. We're painting these walls purple."

"Chief." The man with the sledgehammer shook his head solemnly. "It's a sheer crime is what it is."

"I know. Let me do the hard part for you." Walt grabbed the hammer and swung it into the nearest wood panel. A gaping hole of splintered wood appeared. Walt grabbed the edges around the hole and pulled, tearing out slices of wood and throwing them in the center of the room.

"Ouch," one of his men murmured, then dug his crow-bar around the seams, splitting wood and popping out nails.

Walt returned the tool to its owner and pointed at the wound in the wood. "Spell's broken. Get going."

Shaking his head at the destruction of such a fine room, Walt returned to the garage where other members of his crew had carried the desk. They stood beside it, smoking cigarettes and laughing. Walt was annoyed to find his workers idle.

"Waitin' on keys, Chief," one of them volunteered. "Door's locked."

The gardener appeared like Houdini from behind the garage, swinging a bundle of keys from a rope like a life-guard. Walt had seen the man when he had come to look over the job. He was a middle-aged man with some Hispanic ancestry, judging from his coffee-colored skin and his wide, dark eyes and hair. His face, although wrinkled prematurely by years of working in the sun, was handsome and his eyes sparkled with intelligence and confidence.

"Looking for these?" he asked Walt in a deep, accented voice. Walt noticed that he was taller than he had expected and his arms were sinewy and thick with strength. He had the build of a much younger man.

"Thank you . . ." Walt struggled to remember his name.

"Emmanuel." The gardener smiled, displaying a row of dazzling white teeth. Walt couldn't help but notice a smudge of pink lipstick on the gardener's chin. Emmanuel was fooling around with a lady in the house. Well, none of his business.

Opening the garage door, the men shuffled inside with the desk and placed it against the back wall. Walt then re-joined his crew in the library, where the work on the paneling was going smoothly. A large scrap pile was building in the center of the room. Electrical lines wound like vines from ceiling to floor. He gestured to one of the men to hand over his crowbar.

"Get the wheelbarrow. We've got to clean some of this out of here."

The men worked quickly, joking with one another and sharing stories as they tore out the wood and piled pieces into the wheelbarrow. In the corner of the back wall, Walt dug his crowbar through the panel against the floor. His tool went deep behind the wood, meeting no resistance. Surprised, Walt knelt and began prying the wood away from the initial hole. Instead of seeing the same cracked wall behind the wood, a dark space peered back at him.

"Roy, hand me your flashlight."

"Sure, Chief."

Walt stuck the small face of the flashlight into the hole and switched the light on. The beam fell onto three white shoe boxes, nestled like birds on a nest of newspaper.

"What's that, Chief? Secret hiding spot?"

Walt removed the flashlight and stood. "Yeah, I think so. I'd better get Mrs. Staunton. Don't touch anything."

Walt found Bunny outside, cutting roses. She carried a wide, flat basket and hummed as she selected bright, plump blooms for her arrangements. A large straw hat with a black ribbon masked her face.

"M'am?" Walt called as he approached her.

"Yes?"

"We've found something in your husband's . . . well, inside one of the walls."

Bunny looked at him in confusion. "In the wall?"

"I think you'd better have a look."

Bunny nodded and put her basket down. She followed

Walt quietly into the library, where the noise had ceased and the men stood around in a cluster, waiting.

Walt led Bunny to the hole in the back wall and handed her the flashlight. As she switched on the light, Walt ushered his men out of the room.

"Give her some privacy," he scolded. He was curious too, of course, but made it a rule not to get involved with his client's households. If they wanted to have affairs with the gardener, fine. If they had hidden stashes of drugs or cash, fine. As long as he did his job and got paid for it, they could lead their eccentric lifestyles. He worked in construction, not in therapy or criminal justice.

"Come on, boys. Coffee break."

Bunny reached inside the hole and pulled out the three shoe boxes. She noticed a latch on the panel frame, which must have been the release, hidden to the eye. A person would only need to press the right place and the panel would swing open a crack. Hidden behind a large wing-back chair, no one would have randomly bumped against the spot. No wonder she hadn't known about the existence of a secret panel.

Her hand resting on the dusty lid of the first box, Bunny hesitated. Did she really want to know what was inside? She knew enough of her husband's past as it was. What else was there? Illegitimate children? A secret will?

Bunny sighed, and for the millionth time thought about her life with George-Bradley when they had first been married. They had lived in a quaint townhouse. She had grown vegetables in the small garden out back. He had practiced law and tinkered at his workbench, making wind chimes out of scrap metal. They ate watching television, drank lots of wine, and made love every night. When they moved into this house, bought with the money Bunny inherited from her parents, she thought she was living in a dream.

But the dream slowly faded. Unable to have children, Bunny began growing prize roses obsessively, and George-Bradley began collecting pottery. She took gourmet-cooking classes but her husband was never home to eat her creations. She knew he was seeing other women, and her only comforts became the blue ribbons her roses won and the food she cooked. She put on weight; he stayed downstairs in his wing of the house until bedtime. When he finally got into bed, reeking of cigars and bourbon, he immediately turned away from her and went to sleep. Their only physical contact occurred when Bunny had the pleasure of jabbing her husband in the belly with a small needle twice a day. What had happened to their marriage?

Bunny looked at the gutted walls. The oldest of two children, Bunny had inherited a larger portion of her parent's estate. Her sister, Caroline, had money too, but she never spent any. A spinster, she was a teacher at the nearby middle school. Her retirement was coming up in a few months, and the two sisters decided to meet old age comfortably together in Bunny's house. Bunny wanted to create a separate apartment suite for her sister. She wanted it to be bright and cozy and feminine. No trace of her husband would remain.

There would be no more secrets either. She would tell Caroline that she was in love with Emmanuel. Finally, she would surrender the sham that she had had the perfect marriage. She would drop the role of grieving widow and get rid of all those ridiculous photographs in the living room. People she actually cared about would be placed in those frames.

Taking in a deep breath that tasted of wood and dust, Bunny popped off the lid of the first box. Inside were neat piles of bills, held together with rubber bands and covered in plastic wrap. Bunny saw that they were all stacks of 100s. A few thousand dollars of ready cash, not a bad find.

Relieved, Bunny set the box aside and opened the second. Documents were rolled up neatly inside a plastic tube. Flattening them revealed a pile of bearer bonds, in denominations of $10,000. Bunny counted the bonds. A quarter of a million dollars worth! Why had George-Bradley stashed away all this money? Perhaps he was planning to divorce her so he could get back together with Susan Black. Why else would he hide bonds in a secret panel?

Clutching the papers in anger, Bunny swore.

"He must have been stealing from our account for years! I'd kill that bastard myself if he wasn't already dead."

She stared at the third box.

"Now what, George-Bradley?" she asked the still air. "You haven't done enough to me?"

The third box revealed a solid, heavy lump wrapped in newspaper. Bunny broke through layers of tape and newspaper with her long, sharp nails. Unwrapping the object inside, she stared down at it, perplexed. Gathering the boxes in her hands, she headed back to her wing with a curt nod in the foreman's direction to signal that she had completed her business. He immediately called his men back to work.

Back in her study, Bunny dumped the boxes on her desk. Staring at the object in the third box, she picked up the phone and began dialing.

"At least I know how to get rid of you. You aren't even glazed. Probably worth nothing, just like my husband." She jabbed at it with a scarlet talon, then turned her attention to the voice on the phone. "Lex Lewis, please."

Warmth and sunlight woke the clay. Even through the thick wrapping it could sense the power of release. The clay waited patiently while the folds of newspaper were removed from its curved body. It seemed like eons since its pores last breathed the moving air. Blinded by light, it lay impassive as it allowed the dust to swirl curiously around its form, settling into the round lines of its tail and between the nooks of its paws.

Nails scraped along its body, harshly scratching at its exposed skin, still fragile after so much time alone in the damp dark.

The rabbit was turned upside down. Its ears hung above the ground, listening for the sound of the heavy footsteps of the man who had hidden him away. His scent lingered, but there were other, more recent smells too. The strong tinge of enamel paint, the rubbery smell of caulk, and a brush encrusted with polyurethane. Then there was the scent of the woman. Musky and strong, it spoke to the clay of disguises. It shrank away from the nails and the perfume, turning back to the fading memory of the potter's hands.

The clay was carried off irreverently in one of the woman's hands and then dumped onto the polished surface of a black, lacquered desk. It listened to her voice, brittle and demanding, drift off to another place beyond the room.

"You're not even glazed," her cold voice judged the clay, turning it back and forth dismissively and upside down.

The woman left, taking with her a cloud of anger and disappointment. The quiet crept in on light feet, settling around the clay and soothing it with gentle strokes of emptiness and sunshine.

Outside, a few leaves drifted lazily onto the shady slopes of grass. A thin wisp of air carried a gift of magnolia blossoms and boxwoods to the clay. Yellow finches gathered near the west window, darting flashes of color before the clay's parched eyes. Calmed, it inhaled the summer, the season of its birth.

With the ancient knowledge of the stones and water that had come together to form its heart, the clay knew that someone was coming for it. Someone was coming, someone who had the right hands. It was someone who recognized the spirit of the clay.

The potter was gone and the clay had been alone for a long time now. But soon, very soon, it would be given a home, and a place of honor among the other things birthed from wood and stone and clay. Soon. Soon.

The clay opened up its pores to capture the splinters of wind seeping through the sills. It could wait here for a while. For now, no more darkness would follow.

Chapter 14

But we have this treasure in jars of clay to show that this all-surpassing power is from God and not from us.

—2 Corinthians 4:7

Clara called Molly as she previewed auction items at Bud Earl's Auction Company in Greensboro. As a writer for *Collector's Weekly,* Molly was allowed a private preview. Lingering over a folk art painting of the Statue of Liberty, Molly was so captivated by the bright colors, polka dots, and striped frame that it took her a minute to recognize that the annoying buzzing was coming from her purse.

"Hello?"

"Madam? Are you still at Earl's?" Clara asked.

"I am." Molly moved on to the next painting. It was a primitive work of a black man being chased by an over-sized snake. Simply called "Black Snake" by the artist, it had been painted on a piece of pine that had once served as part of an outhouse door.

Yesterday's threatening voice mail had almost faded in

light of the lively folk art and the warm memory of Mark's kiss, which she replayed in her mind again and again.

"He have anything good?" Clara broke into her reverie.

"Some great folk art," Molly confessed sheepishly. After all, other auction companies were competition for Lex.

"Can you do Lex and me a huge favor?" Clara asked.

"What is it?"

"Bunny found one more piece of George-Bradley's pottery. Would you mind picking it up? I've got an appraisal in Raleigh so I'll be too busy to get it."

Molly was a bit apprehensive about seeing Bunny after witnessing her face-off with Susan, but she was halfway to Asheboro already. Still, she could use this opportunity to dig more information up on the Stauntons' marriage and George-Bradley's last morning alive. Molly was certain she'd get some kind of vibe about whether or not Bunny was guilty of murder. Maybe she'd even learn more about the mysterious letter. "Sure," she told Clara charitably. "What is the piece?"

"Don't know, but she said it wasn't glazed, so it's no keeper."

"Good, I'll offer her $10 for it," Molly joked.

"Go ahead. Lex doesn't even want it. It won't fit in with the rest of the collection we're auctioning next month. And after all the money we got for that woman for the first group she didn't seem the least bit grateful."

Molly paused. "It's not the money, Ma. The pottery just held bad memories for her. She just wants to be done with it."

"As *we* want to be done with her. Thanks." Clara rang off.

Stuffing her phone back in her purse, Molly finished viewing the artwork. Earl had over two dozen primitive folk art paintings from a variety of North Carolina artists. Folk art was becoming a hot item across the East Coast. She decided to write an introductory piece about folk art in addition to her article on the auction. She hoped Swanson would approve. Taking down some notes on several of the artists, she thanked the auctioneer and headed once more for Bunny's house.

After ringing the doorbell for the third time, Molly let out a sigh of frustration. Clearly, no one was going to answer. Through the front window, she could see a shoe box propped on the hall table with the words *Lex Lewis* marked on it. She tried the door. It was unlocked.

Tiptoeing over to the small box stuffed with paper, Molly picked it up and carefully peeled back the folds of tissue and saw the face of a clay rabbit peering up at her from its white nest. It had been fired, but not yet glazed.

The little rabbit, with its winking eyes and long, pert ears smiled up at her. She delicately traced its incised whiskers and felt the curve of its graceful hind leg. She stroked the two front paws and ran her fingertips lovingly down its arched back.

"Hello," she whispered to it.

Carefully tipping the rabbit upside down, she searched for initials. What she saw made her suck in her breath in a great gasp.

"Jack Graham. Kiln #43." She looked back into the rabbit's eyes and exhaled in awe. "My God. You're a piece from the missing kiln."

She cradled the clay piece in her hands, cupping its body as if it were a tiny sparrow fallen from the nest.

Suddenly the silence in the room seemed to lengthen.

The birdsong and insect buzzing faded. She held the rabbit to her and felt the life within the clay. She knew of its journey through the riverbed, saw the spinning wheel slick with water, the potter's hands, and felt the night curl around it as it dried in the summer air.

"Poor thing, you've been in the dark all this time. Don't worry, that's all over now. You're coming home with me."

Suddenly, in a house that moments ago seemed completely empty, a piercing scream erupted.

"Nnnooooooooooo!" echoed a man's voice filled with pain.

Molly jumped up and ran into Bunny's wing, the rabbit still clutched in her hand.

At first all she saw was the gardener on his knees, rocking back and forth and screaming. As she reached out to touch him, she saw Bunny.

Bunny was laid out on the sofa as if she had swooned, her yellow blouse torn through the center of her chest where a bullet had bit through the fabric. Blood was splattered in thin droplets all over the white sofa and wall. More blood had dripped from her back and pooled onto the hardwood floor. The gardener was kneeling in it as he held Bunny's limp hand and wailed.

A pink pillow lay at Bunny's feet, its fibrous filling scattered over her legs and the floor. Whoever had killed Bunny had shot her at close range through the pillow.

Molly blinked, disbelieving what her eyes were telling her. She stared dumbly at the red blood pooled by her shoe. Bunny was dead, right in front of her. She took a step back, shaking herself out of shock.

Her first action was to stop the gardener from screaming. She grabbed his shoulder and shook him.

"What's your name?" she demanded firmly.

The man turned his coffee-colored eyes to her without seeing. "I am . . . my name is Emmanuel."

"Come away, Emmanuel," she said more gently, tugging at his arm to get him to stand up. When he wouldn't budge, she pulled him harder. "We have to call the police. Please, come."

Mindlessly he stood and followed her. His yelling had turned to weeping, and Molly instinctively put her arm around his waist·and propelled him to the kitchen. After calling the police and reporting the murder, she put the kettle on and searched in the cupboards until she found packets of tea.

"I'm sorry," she said a few minutes later as she poured Emmanuel a strong cup of tea. "Drink this, it will help calm you down. Do you think you can you tell me what happened?"

Emmanuel took a deep sip and looked at her as tears ran down his cheeks. "I don't know. I just . . . found her. Someone shot her. I was outside so I never heard the shot." He shook his head. "I loved her, but they will think I did it. I am the gardener! A foreigner! They will—"

"No one will think you did it," Molly cut him off before he became hysterical. "Do you even own a gun?"

"No," Emmanuel replied tonelessly.

"Well, that's a good start in proving your innocence. Were there any guns in the house?"

"Mr. Staunton owned some old shotguns. All his stuff is gone now though."

"Did you see anyone around the house this morning?" Molly asked. "Any cars come down the driveway?"

Emmanuel tried to concentrate. "I was working by the tennis court most of day. I can't see much from back there and I was using the hedge trimmers. They are very loud.

All I know is Bunny was expecting someone to pick up *el conejo*."

Molly didn't recognize the Spanish word. "The what?"

"The rabbit." He gestured at the pottery figure standing on the kitchen counter.

"That was me." Molly sighed. "No other cars?"

Emmanuel buried his face in his hands. Molly thought he would begin crying again, but he suddenly looked up at her with dry, bright eyes. "I did see one! I don't know cars, but it was white."

"And big, more like a van instead of a car?"

"Si, yes, higher than a car." He raised his hand up.

At that moment, the police burst into the front hall. An officer strode into the kitchen and asked to be shown the body. Remarkably calm, Molly directed Emmanuel to stay put and led the police to Bunny's sitting room.

As she explained her presence to the officer in charge, a Mr. Bennett, Emmanuel was led through the halls, his shoulders drooping as the two officers prodded him forward.

"I tell you!" he moaned. "I loved her! I did not kill her!"

"If you're innocent," one of the policemen said calmly, "the evidence will prove it."

"Will you need an interpreter?" the second one asked unkindly. Emmanuel ignored him.

Bennett quickly intervened, warning his men to keep their mouths shut before turning curious eyes to Molly. "I thought you were just picking up a piece of pottery. You sound like you may have an idea who the killer is."

Molly thought about the threatening voice mail and shivered. Then she grew angry. How dare someone try to scare her? She would make them sorry.

She returned Bennett's gaze and surprised him by saying, "Not just an idea. I absolutely know who the killer is."

* * *

Bennett called for a police car to apprehend the suspect and meet him back at the station. He told Molly she would have to come to the station as well to fill out a report.

Holding Emmanuel with gentle firmness by the arm, Bennett gave orders to the forensic unit and to the coroner before escorting Molly and Emmanuel to his car.

"Bennett!" an officer called after him. "Let me swab those two for residue."

"Residue?" Molly asked.

"Gunpowder," Bennett replied and nodded at the officer. "Go ahead, Frank."

Both Molly and Emmanuel's hands were swabbed. Frank shook his head and turned back to help his crew unload equipment.

"No traces on either of you," Bennett explained, holding open the car door.

At the small police station, Molly was given an awful cup of coffee and some stale cheese crackers while she made her statement. There were only a few rooms aside from the cells so Molly and Emmanuel were seated at tables next to one another. Bennett sat across from Molly and asked questions as another officer took notes on a pad.

She calmly explained her reasons for being at the Staunton place as well as how she knew the identity of the killer. The only thing about the experience that unnerved her was the presence of the tape recorder on the table.

"Just try to ignore it," Bennett suggested, watching Molly stare at the spinning disks inside the recorder.

As she was in the middle of describing the voice mail message she had received, an officer led a petite woman clad in a black pantsuit into the station. When the woman's angry gaze fell upon Molly, she lurched free of the man's grip, grabbed a stapler off the nearest desk, and ran straight for her.

"You fat, nosy bitch! I'll kill you too!" Susan Black screamed.

Bennett rose and intercepted her raised hand in a quick, fluid motion. Susan fumed and struggled beneath his iron grasp, her eyes never leaving Molly's face.

"It was MY money! MINE! I deserved it for sleeping with that disgusting bastard! For keeping his stupid secrets! I deserved it ALL! And you, you nosy BITCH . . . !" Susan was dragged away, spitting and yelling every obscenity Molly had ever heard until the doors to the cells clanked behind her.

Bennett sank back into his chair, took a sip of coffee, and grimaced.

"Awful swill. Please continue with your statement, Miss Appleby."

By dinnertime, Molly was luxuriating in a dip in Clara's hot tub with a large pína colada in one hand.

Clara hovered nearby, uncharacteristically ruffled by her daughter's explanation of the day's events.

Finally, Molly scolded Clara until she settled into a nearby lounge chair, making room for her favorite cat, a twenty-two-pound apricot-colored tabby named Tiny Purr. She began sipping rapidly from a crystal tumbler filled with Crown Royal and water.

"Doesn't look like you've got much water in there, Ma," Molly teased.

"Hah! You're lucky there's even any ice in here. I don't

know how you can settle for a tutti-frutti drink at a time like this. Poor Bunny! And my poor Baby Girl!"

"You know sugar makes everything alright for me. I'm tired, but at least this mystery is almost solved," Molly said as she sank deeper into the warm water.

"Oh, there can't be anymore surprises left. Susan killed them both. She must have! She was at the kiln opening and she hated both the Stauntons," Clara said with finality.

"We'll see what Officer Bennett comes up with. Now . . . look in that box." Molly pointed to a side table. "That's the piece of pottery I went to pick up."

Molly watched as her mother lifted the rabbit from the box. Her own feelings of discovery were mirrored on her mother's face as her jaw slacked with shock.

"Kiln #43! I can't believe it!"

"Isn't he beautiful?" Molly said proudly.

"He is. He's wonderful." Her mother looked at her. "So there *was* a surviving kiln load. But what happened to the rest of the pieces?"

"I don't know. I need to find out more about Jack Graham."

Clara held the rabbit up triumphantly, her worries vanishing like the ice in her drink. "Well, you'll have the chance next weekend."

"How?"

Clara produced a postcard, which she had been using as a bookmark and smiled widely. "Jack Graham is having his first kiln opening in two years. It's a small, private affair for a select group of friends and collectors."

"How did you get your hands on an invitation?" Molly asked.

"Donald, of course."

"That man is a wonder," Molly said.

The two women sat in silence, admiring the pottery rabbit that basked in the glow of the waning summer sun.

Molly dried off and picked up the rabbit, gazing at it with maternal tenderness.

"Only one question remains. If that kiln wasn't supposed to exist, how did George-Bradley get ahold of you?"

Chapter 15

Clay. It's rain, dead leaves, dust, all my dead ancestors. Stones that have been ground into sand. Mud. The whole cycle of life and death.

—MARTINE VERMEULEN

"Do tell, Miss Marple. Was Susan Black really wearing gold lamé shoes when she was arrested? I have a bet with Francis over it." Clayton leaned a hip clad in suede jeans on Molly's desk.

She tried to remember. "Yes, I think she was."

"Lord have mercy! Who does she think she is, Tina Turner? Now I owe Francis a dinner at Café Luna. Damn. Oopsie, time to run." Clayton jumped up and scurried away as Mark came out of his office carrying a huge bouquet of wildflowers.

"These are for you." He smiled and laid them on her desk. "The hero of the hour. Or . . . er . . . heroine, I guess. Feel up to going to lunch?"

"Absolutely. Thank you." Molly's stomach rumbled in anticipation. "Let's go," she laughed.

Later, settled at a cozy table at a small, Italian eatery, Molly told Mark all about her visit to Bunny's.

"How did you know the killer was Susan Black?" Mark asked as they buttered slices of warm, crusty bread.

"I saw her car at the auction. A white Mercedes SUV. I wondered where she had gotten the money for that car, the pottery, and her clothes. She has no regular job that I know of. I guess George-Bradley had treated her well when they were together and she didn't want to stop living the good life."

"But didn't you say they had been broken up for awhile?" Mark asked, twirling spaghetti in meat sauce around on his fork.

"Yeah, but there was that thing Bunny whispered in Susan's ear about the car ride in the backwoods. I guess I'll never know everything Bunny said or what was in that letter, but it was enough to get her killed."

"And seeing the body didn't bother you?"

Molly cut one of her herbed meatballs in two and sent sauce flying onto the white tablecloth. "Oops." She colored. "Sorry, I've never been good at eating Italian without getting sauce somewhere. Did seeing Bunny bother me? No, it didn't. She didn't seem like a real person anymore, you know? She was more like a wax figure from Madame Tussauds."

"That's the way it was in med school too. I was pretty nervous about my first anatomy class, but it wasn't that bad. The cadavers weren't like real people anymore. They were more like CPR dummies. At least it helped to think of them that way."

Molly looked up at him. "Can I ask you why you didn't finish?"

Mark peered at her defensively, and then his face softened. "Yes. It's just painful to talk about. In the summer before my last year, my parents were killed in a car accident." He paused and took a deep drink of Chianti. "I had to take care of all the arrangements—it was just my younger brother and me—and by the time the estate was straightened out, school had started and I wasn't ready to go back . . ."

"Of course you weren't. I'm so sorry, Mark." Molly covered his hand with hers.

"I might go back someday. I still want to be a doctor," Mark said as he squeezed her hand in return, "but I can't see leaving work now when I have such good company there."

"Are you going to quit?" Swanson barked at Molly after lunch.

"Why?" she asked, horrified that her piece on Sam Chance might have been poorly written.

"Because you seem more involved with hard-boiled crime stories these days than reporting on antiques and collectibles. I want a piece that finishes this pottery series off with a bang."

Molly squirmed as Swanson's foul breath hit her in the face. "I *have* found one more potter I'd like to interview."

"And perhaps you'd like to tell me who."

"His name is Jack Graham. He's another Seagrove potter, but Sam Chance said he doesn't do interviews anymore."

"Any reason?" Swanson's curiosity was roused.

Molly repeated Sam's words and the manner in which he refused to give out any information aside from warning her to stay away. Swanson's eyes lit up at the thought of a dramatic secret adding more spice to the paper. The recent edition, filled with details on George-Bradley's death and

Hillary Keane's arrest had created record highs in circulation.

"You get that interview with Graham. I don't care how you get it, just get it." He broke off to cough up something liquid into his yellowed handkerchief.

"Yes," Molly said, backing away from the desk in disgust. "I'll try to get something lined up with him this weekend."

But before the weekend's kiln opening, she needed to find out more about this potter whose only surviving piece from an entire kiln had been a small rabbit.

The next day, Molly headed for the library at Duke University, an old, gray stone building with Tudor-style windows and a sprawling layout of endless rooms. The atmosphere was both quiet and lively.

As posters of Lincoln, Harriet Tubman, and the Wright Brothers cast knowing but affable glances down upon her, she began searching through databases for newspaper articles on Jack Graham.

Scanning through the summary lines on the computer screen she noted that most of these were articles about the uniqueness of his work or short pieces reviewing his kiln openings. His name popped up in several other searches relating to the Seagrove area and its potters, but nothing appeared about his personal life.

Molly read everything available to her, printing out a few of the articles reviewing Graham's work in order to improve her own knowledge of the talented craftsman. Nothing indicated the Graham had faced any "trouble," but then again, none of the articles mentioned anything personal about Graham except for his age and the family's history of pottery making. Stumped, Molly approached the reference desk to seek help.

A tall, pale-faced librarian with a white button-down shirt and frayed brown pants greeted her kindly. His round, thick glasses enlarged his greenish eyes and enunciated his hooked nose, giving the impression of a friendly turtle. There was nothing slow about his fingers, however, and when Molly explained what she was looking for, his hands flew like startled finches over the keys.

"Jack Graham," he said, lips crinkling in concentration, "a Seagrove potter, if I'm not mistaken."

"Yes."

"Known for his perfect form and the brilliant hues of his glazes," he continued.

"Yes." Molly was impressed.

"The Archives Database will provide birth information, so you'll know his age and place of birth, but that's not much." His fingers continued to peck at the keyboard. "Let's see what the local press has to say."

Results danced over the screen in black and blue lines of text. The librarian did not seem pleased. He sighed heavily, stroking the gray stubble peppering his chin.

"Once again, progress is halted due to lack of funding."

"What happened?" Molly asked, disappointed. Mr. Turtle seemed as capable as a magician waving his wand over a black hat. She had expected those nimble fingers to pull out the white rabbit of news articles on the life of Jack Graham.

"The microfiche of the Asheboro papers, which would have covered all events occurring in Seagrove, have not been downloaded into the database yet. Their branch needs to link with our database, but they only have one or two computers. The state has made huge cuts from library budgets everywhere. The smaller libraries are really suffering." He shrugged. "Remember this for the next election year."

"So if they can't afford to have the database, are all the area newspaper articles on microfiche?"

"Probably, yes. I'm afraid you'll have to go to the main branch in Asheboro and look at films the old-fashioned way."

Molly thanked Mr. Turtle for his help, and then headed for the interstate. She'd have a quick lunch then drive the hour and a half to Asheboro once again. She stopped on the way at a cafeteria and selected an array of homemade foods for lunch, including macaroni and cheese, black-eyed peas, and bread pudding with vanilla custard sauce for dessert.

The librarian at the local branch was an older woman with curly, paper-white hair, so thin that her pink scalp winked out in places like bare patches in the lawn. Her eyes were sharp blue and sparkled with vivacity. She patted Molly on the hand after listening to her request and handed her several old index boxes.

"These are the newspaper films we've got on file. You just find out what issue you want and bring the card up here. I'll get the films and set you up on the reader."

"Thank you." Molly made herself comfortable in an oversized pink chair by the window and began flipping through the cards. Each card contained a summary of the important articles of the week, sorted by subject. She began flipping through the "Arts" sections, musing over the difference between Duke's database and this library's boxes of yellow aged index cards.

As the afternoon wore on, Molly found several references to Jack Graham's work. She had a small stack of

cards laid aside with short articles covering his kiln openings. As the librarian leaned over her to line up the rolls of
microfiche, Molly caught a sweet, familiar whiff of vanilla.
Molly always burned vanilla candles in her house, and her
favorite coffee flavor was French vanilla.

"Anything wrong, dear?" the librarian's mellifluous
voice asked.

"Not at all," she assured the librarian. "You smell
lovely."

Molly scrolled through pages of film, printing out any
articles where Jack Graham's name appeared. She then
collected her pile of printouts and returned to her soft chair
to read, hoping at least to learn wo what buyers were present at each sale. Would any of these short pieces hold clues
about Graham's personal life?

Most of the articles were about Graham's pieces being
exhibited in the area museums or about his biannual kiln
openings. Molly began by numbering the articles on the
openings, so she could discover what month kiln number
43 had *not* been produced. She paused over any photographs from the sales, noting familiar figures such as
George-Bradley, Hillary Keane, Clara's friend Donald, and
even Clara herself. Most of these were taken before the
kiln opening began, when frenzied buyers stood with their
hands resting on the piece of their choice, carefully guard-
ing it until the time they could check out.

By kiln number 25, Molly noticed that Jack Graham
had switched to the lottery system. Now photos showed
buyers drawing from a hat and studying their numbers with
glee or dismay. Those with low numbers picked first,
snatching the most singular pieces from the sale. By the
end of the lottery, only a few plain vases or ordinary bowls
remained. They were all beautiful, but not as unique as the

one peacock-incised floor vase or elaborate salt-glazed candelabra that the lucky holders of low lottery numbers had seized in the first few rounds of drawings.

In fact, one photo illustrated a woman throwing her hands in the air in disgust as she discovered what number she had drawn. Molly smiled at the photo, as it was so typical of the emotions displayed all over in the world of collecting. She examined the article further, admiring a photo of neat rows of pottery in Graham's yard, the words of praise from the local museum curators, and the attendance his work drew for county festivals. So far, Graham's life seemed trouble free.

As she continued to number the articles, the late afternoon sun began to grow weary and rested its weighty head among the pines dotting the horizon. The librarian hummed at her desk, her small hands flipping through the pages of a colorful children's book. Molly watched her, wondering if she would know anything more about Graham. After all, she had probably lived in the area for a long time and if there were any noteworthy personal information about him, surely a local person would know.

"M'am?" she interrupted the librarian's reading.

"Can I help you, dear?"

"I can't seem to find what I'm looking for," Molly said truthfully.

"Those films didn't help?" the bright eyes asked in sympathy.

"No. I'm looking for information on Jack Graham, the potter. Do you know him?"

The woman's wrinkled forehead gathered into itself as she thought. "I've heard of him, yes. He makes pottery, but not much these days I hear."

Molly showed her the numbered stack of articles.

"About two years ago, in the spring, he should have had kiln opening number 43, but he didn't. I'm trying to figure out why."

"Well, let me see." The librarian shuffled back over to the drawers holding the microfiche. "We'll have to look at that year's events some more. Maybe there was a fire or something . . . some catastrophe that prevented him from working."

Molly digested the librarian's comment, and then seized upon an idea. "Fire, maybe . . . or snow!" she suggested, excitedly. "Isn't that the winter we had those two big storms back-to-back and no one had power for weeks?"

"It is, it is." The blue eyes sparkled.

"And he might not have been able to work without power," Molly continued.

The librarian loaded in the film, and the two women sat side by side and read about the aftermath of the two blizzards. North Carolina rarely saw snow, and when it came, it was usually a light dusting that sent people dashing out to the store for bread, milk, and eggs. Driving conditions were bad because the state had no equipment for snow removal. Still, people who could barely drive well in rain went racing off in a state of panic to the grocer's, causing dozens of accidents each time a cluster of snowflakes flew.

But the blizzards were different. They each piled six to eight inches of snow in some places, downing power lines and covering the roads completely. After the two storms had dumped their loads of heavy powder, a rain had fallen, covering the world in a clear layer of sparkling, treacherous ice.

Molly remembered using her gas logs to stay warm and sleeping on the sofa for a week. With no electricity, she had to reread all of Jane Austen's novels and put together puzzles by candlelight, thrilled at having a week off school and enjoying the adventure of donning snow gear to walk a mile to the grocery store where she waited for two hours in line to buy cat food and granola bars.

However, she lived in a populated development, and by the second week her power was restored, and even though her car was snowed in, she could walk fairly easily to the store and could make phone calls to her friends and family. Others had not been so lucky.

Out in the country, many people had no source of energy except for small, wood-burning stoves. They had no access to grocery stores and had to rely on whatever canned goods were at hand. Dozens of fatalities occurred from car accidents. Worse than that, several people had died from hypothermia when they got trapped in the high snow heading to town on the remote back roads. When the snow melted, their bodies were discovered near the road or lying down in their cars, where they had gotten stuck too far from town and too far from home.

"Maybe that's it." Molly turned to her helper, thinking about the news stories she had seen on TV about the serious conditions people in the country faced during those two weeks. "What about that storm could have changed Jack Graham's life? A friend of mine told me that the family had had some trouble. Did they . . . did he lose someone in that storm?"

The librarian didn't answer. She seemed lost in thought.

"Ma'am?"

"Oh," the woman said and flashed her a smile. "I was just trying to remember. And call me Harriet, dear. There's something scratching at my brain but I can't figure out what it is. We can check the obituaries for the months before Graham was supposed to have his opening. He had one in the spring and one in the fall, correct?" Molly nodded. "But we've got to shake a tail feather because it's almost closing time," the librarian added.

Molly looked at her watch in alarm. She only had twenty minutes left. If she didn't find something today, she'd have to make the hour and a half trip again after the auction this weekend.

"Don't fret." Harriet held out two rolls of fresh film. "You check the months you have and I'll look back in the October and November obituaries."

"Thank you, that's very kind."

The two women fell silent, scanning the names of those who had died between October and April, looking for a familiar name or face to jump out from where it was buried in positives and negatives within the screen. Graham's openings were regularly held in September and April, early in the morning on vibrant, crisp days. Molly was loading in the film for February when Harriet gasped beside her.

"What is it?" Molly asked.

"I'm remembering." The blue eyes shifted slowly from the screen to the sinking sun out the window. "There was something about one of his children."

"I read in a biographical piece that he had two."

"Something," Harriet said as she turned back to her machine and began hastily loading in the October film. "There was something about his little girl."

Molly abandoned her machine and slid her chair closer to Harriet's, comforted by her vanilla scent and the fruity perfumes of her hair.

Suddenly, Molly felt a strong foreboding grip her. They were about to uncover something horrible, something that shouldn't be discovered by a stranger.

Molly found she no longer wanted to know what happened to disturb the balance of this man's life. He was a gifted potter, a husband, and a father. What was she doing here, searching for his secrets? It was his life; his reasons for taking a season off of pottery making were his own. She was no tabloid journalist.

Shaken, she reached out to tell Harriet to stop, that it didn't matter, that there were others to interview, that she had been wrong to come. Her hand reached out, touched the soft fabric of Harriet's cotton blouse, and rested there.

"Here!" Harriet breathed, arresting the words on Molly's lips.

She pointed to an obituary toward the middle of the first column. Hesitating, Molly looked at the photograph of a smiling little girl with long pigtail braids tied with gingham bows. She was missing one of her front teeth and large dimples dented her shiny cheeks. She wore a jumper over a T-shirt and looked impatient to be on the move again yet too good-natured not to smile sweetly for what must have been a school picture. Molly read:

Graham

Lilly Ann Graham, age 9, departed this life Saturday, October 3rd to join the Lord. She is survived by her loving parents, Jack and Leslie Graham and by her brother Jack Junior, age 7. Lilly Ann was in the third grade at Seagrove Elementary School where she excelled in art and science classes. She played competitive soccer and recently starred in her class play, *Many Moons*. Lilly Ann will be remembered for her loving, generous spirit. Memorial services will be held Monday, October 5th from noon until one

at the Piney Hollow Methodist Church, 1500
North Bramble Drive. Interment will be at the
Seagrove Memorial Cemetery. In lieu of flowers,
the family suggests contributions to be made to
The Girl Scouts of America, of which Lilly Ann
was an enthusiastic member.

Molly sat back in her chair, her hand covering her
mouth. What had happened to Graham's little girl?

"How horrible," she muttered, blinking back tears as
she stared at Lilly Ann's face. "That poor family."

Harriet turned to her, blue eyes liquid as they reflected
the light from the screen. "Now I remember," she whispered, then turned back to the machine and went back to
the front page of the same edition. "Look."

Molly felt a shiver ripple up her arms. One of the bold
headlines read, "Seagrove Girl Killed By Hit-and-Run."

"They found her in the road," Harriet began, speaking
so softly that Molly could barely hear her. "She was already dead. She had been riding her bike . . . I remember
that. Here's a picture of it, see?" Molly unwillingly leaned
forward to see the crushed and twisted metal remains. Harriet continued, "I remember her mother telling a reporter
that she never let Lilly Ann go too far from home. She had
some kind of medical condition. She was allowed to ride
down to the creek in one direction and to the neighbor's in
the other. That day, she was going to the creek to sail some
paper boats she'd made at school. They were still in her
backpack."

"How awful," Molly said sadly.

"They never caught the driver. He hit her and ran off
with no witnesses to the scene. Back where most of those
potters live, there aren't too many other folks around."

Harriet sighed, turning away from the tragic headline. "That was the worst of it . . . that whoever killed this sweet little girl probably never stopped, never even pulled over to see if she was alive."

"And no one was ever arrested?" Molly asked in disbelief.

"No one." Harriet closed her eyes for a moment. "He got away. But his time will come. That's the way things work in this world."

Molly was stunned. As Harriet pressed the "print" button and noiselessly moved off to begin her closing tasks, she remained immobile in her wooden chair. Finally, as the humming of the machines clicked off to silence, Molly let her head sink into her hands, her eyes straying to the window.

At last, all of the pieces of the puzzle about George-Bradley's death fell together. Molly now knew who the killer was. What should have been a triumphant moment filled her with a heavy weariness. And she would still need to prove herself right before mentioning what she knew to anyone else.

The surrendering sun had disappeared behind the blue black line of trees and long snakelike shadows crept like tendrils across the library floor. The other people who had been reading or typing at computers had gone. The fluorescent lights fizzled and strained to make up for the departure of natural light. Molly turned full circle before her stack of paper and note cards, searching for a sign of life.

But she was alone with no comfort left in the dying day.

Chapter 16

Potters have always catered to children—in part, because children have always been drawn to their shops to witness the magical growth of a jug on the wheel or to take part in the excitement of kiln burning.

—CHARLES G. ZUG III, FROM *TURNERS AND BURNERS*

Jack Graham's kiln opening for kiln number 50 took place under a rented tent in his backyard at the reasonable hour of ten o'clock on a fine, late summer morning. Two picnic tables held the seventy-five extraordinary pieces of pottery to be sold before lunch.

Driving with Clara and Donald, Molly kept opening the shoe box on her lap to gaze sadly upon the face of her little rabbit. She planned to return him to the Grahams, the rightful owners, and hopefully put an end to all the mystery that had begun just a few weeks ago at another kiln opening.

"So tell Donald why Susan Black killed Bunny. He hasn't heard the whole story," Clara prompted from the front seat.

Molly took a sip of creamy hazelnut coffee. "One of my coworkers, Clayton, gets all the juicy tidbits from a friend of his from the *Times*. Apparently, Susan knew all about the bearer bonds George-Bradley had stashed away and was waiting for the right time to steal them from the house. Her plan was to grab the certificates and leave the state. That's why she never called me back to schedule an interview."

"I take it Bunny didn't oblige her," Donald stated.

"I guess not. Susan claimed that George-Bradley had been saving that money so that once he and Bunny were divorced, he could start a new life with her. He told Susan about his hiding place in the wall but Susan didn't count on Bunny being home. That was Bunny's regular day to play bridge at her sister's house, but she had changed her schedule in order to meet Lex. Of course, it was me who came, not Lex."

"But Susan had a gun with her!" Clara exclaimed.

"Yes, and when the police picked her up she was loading a box of pottery into her car. She had fake identification papers and was planning to live a quiet life of ease in the Caymans. She also showed no signs of remorse. She felt she was owed those bonds, and she was going to get them no matter what."

Donald shook his head. "But they had broken up two years ago, so *now* she decides to go after this money?"

Molly shrugged. "I guess she figured with George-Bradley dead, she could take the bonds and no one would be the wiser. Susan knew where the bearer bonds were hidden and she must have figured that Bunny knew nothing about the secret panel. So she took a chance and went to get them without thinking about the consequences of getting caught. However, Susan did not seem like a stable person in the police station. I mean, who tries to kill someone with a stapler?"

"I'm glad *you* can be so flippant about that," Clara complained. "As for your poor mother . . . the images I have from your recent events! How can you get yourself in the middle of such a mess? If you were at home with a few children to keep you busy—"

"Anyway," Molly interrupted as Donald winked at her through the rearview mirror, "it looks like Bunny's estate, which is worth over three million dollars, will be divided between her sister and Emmanuel." Molly paused and smiled, thinking of Emmanuel's kind, weathered face. "When I last talked to Officer Bennett, he told me that Susan confessed to killing Bunny but refused to admit that she left me a voice mail message."

"Ah well," Clara said dismissively, "you said yourself she wasn't stable. Look at all that rage she kept inside."

"Well that's that," Donald pronounced. "Now, what about our friend, Hillary? Any news on that front?"

"Actually, Clayton told me that Mr. Keane is facing a long jail sentence. Apparently he has been stealing pottery from both potters and collectors for years and selling it to buyers up north. He was dashing off to a rendezvous in Hendersonville to sell a huge inventory of stolen pieces when he almost hit that jogger."

"What?" Clara shrieked. "I thought he was just taking pieces from George-Bradley now and then."

"No, he has been stealing pottery for years. He even stole pieces from three area museums. The FBI's Antiquity Recovery Division is very pleased to have him in jail. Keane still had the museum pieces in his garage, and now they are proudly back on display in their rightful homes."

"But that still doesn't explain his motives," Clara said.

"Pure greed, Ma. You know how it is in the world of collecting. Keane wanted the big house, the period furniture, and a prime pottery collection, but his salary as a small-town pharmacist couldn't finance his dreams. In fact, he has a famous nickname on the Internet."

"What was that?" Donald asked expectantly.

"The Pirate of Pottery," Molly said.

"I just can't believe it," Clara muttered. "You think you know someone. He seemed the very portrait of a gentleman on the outside. All that time envy was burning a hole in him on the inside. Who would have thought?"

Molly looked down at the rabbit. "Some people are really good at hiding their true feelings."

Jack Graham was stocky, muscular, and completely bald. One weathered hand rhythmically stroked his short brown beard as he waited for everyone to take their seats. Molly noticed that there were more people present than there were pieces of pottery. Folks had come to welcome the Grahams back to their old life of public kiln openings. It had been over two years since they had had an open sale. Molly recognized several local potters as well as a member of the local press.

"Thank y'all for comin'." Jack hushed the crowd with a soft, commanding voice. "Just so there's no question of cheatin', Jack Junior is gonna pass the 'Numbers Hat' today. When you hear your number called, go on up and pick your piece. We've got some folks to help you wrap it when you're ready to go. Please help yourself to some fried chicken and biscuits too. Leslie's been cooking all morning."

The crowd applauded as Jack's wife Leslie blushed at

the attention. Molly recognized her from C. C.'s kiln opening. She had helped Eileen serve the sweet tea and cookies.

With a clear view, Molly could now see that Leslie was well into her second trimester of pregnancy. Her long, auburn hair and freckled face glowed with anticipation. How happy she must be to see her husband back at work and to be expecting another child.

Molly knew that no parent ever finishes grieving over a lost child, and both the Grahams had trace amounts of sadness in their eyes and buried in the lines on their cheeks. Nine-year-old dimpled Jack Junior, on the other hand, bounded around the buyers, letting them draw numbered tickets from a battered top hat.

"I forgot to mention," Donald cleared his throat as Jack Junior headed their way and slid a postcard into Molly's hand, "Blake can't make the sale so you can use his card to get a number."

Molly's eyes grew round in wonder and she planted a kiss on Donald's cheek. "Thank you, Donald!"

Clara beamed at her friend. "You are a prince among frogs!" she said as she patted Donald on the arm.

Jack Junior reached Clara first and she put her hand in his deep hat and took a ticket. Donald drew next. Then, it was Molly's turn to pick.

"Donald!" Clara quickly exclaimed. "How did you get so lucky?"

Donald slyly showed Molly his ticket. He had drawn the number 3. He would be the third person to pick a piece of pottery. His eyes gleamed in excitement and relief. Clara had drawn number 32, and Molly had drawn number 50. She certainly wasn't disappointed, as she hadn't expected to own a piece at all.

Excitement began to build as the numbers were handed out. Unlike C. C.'s opening, there was no hostility between the buyers. No one had to race to seize the piece they wanted. This was all left to chance, so there was no one to get angry with except for the fates. Everyone seemed pleased to simply be present and witness Jack Graham's return to the public eye.

As Donald's number was called, he carefully walked up to a pair of tall candlesticks glazed in red brown, each encircled by a green and black striped snake. Molly waited until her mother had chosen a large white and brown swirled serving bowl. Clara reminded Molly that the swirls came from using two types of clay and that it was extremely difficult to create even spirals when mixing clays. Jack Graham's swirls had turned out perfectly.

Molly handed her number to her mother.

"Will you pick for me?" she asked quietly, her mind on other matters.

"Sure, but why?" Clara asked, surprised.

"I want a word with Leslie while people are busy picking," Molly explained and excused herself.

She made her way to the back porch of the Graham's house where Leslie sat watching the next buyer deliberate over two of her husband's pieces. Molly introduced herself, and as Leslie stood to shake her hand, Jack Junior interrupted and begged for a soda before lunch.

"Not now, Jack. Those drinks are for the guests. You can have some juice or milk from in the house."

Sulking, Jack flopped down from the porch and went to hang over the food table.

"You'd think I never fed that boy." Leslie smiled indulgently as she watched her son. She turned to Molly. "I've read your pieces in *Collector's Weekly*. I think you've done some good for the potters around here. I think Sam Chance has gotten some extra business."

"I sure hope so," Molly replied, flattered. Leslie was one of those rare individuals people liked immediately. Perhaps it was her sprinkling of freckles or her lively green eyes, but Molly felt completely at ease with her. "Do you think I could get an interview with your husband sometime this week?"

Leslie paused. "Yes, I think you could. We could use the publicity now that he's back in business. Oh!" she exclaimed, putting a hand on her belly.

"Are you all right?"

"Yes. It was just a kick and a hard one too! Come on in to the kitchen and we'll check the calendar. With all Jack Junior's baseball and soccer games, we have to plan our lives around him."

"How far along are you?" Molly asked as they went inside the shotgun-style house.

"Twenty-four weeks and counting," Leslie said, rubbing her lower back.

"Do you know what you're having?"

"Yes, another boy." Leslie smiled at Molly. "Another soccer player too, I'd say. I hardly slept a wink last night. Please sit down."

Molly laughed. Then she remembered the shoe box she was carrying. "Oh, I have something that I believe rightfully belongs to you."

Leslie looked up from the calendar she was holding and eyed the shoe box warily. "To me?"

"Well, to your family . . ." Molly faltered. She unwrapped the rabbit so that it could explain itself.

Leslie's face turned pale. A hand fluttered up to her chest. She seemed on the point of flight, but changed her mind and with a deep breath, sank down in a chair next to Molly.

She touched the rabbit's face as tears sprang into her eyes.

"A little gift for my daughter," she whispered, looking down at the piece. "She was killed by a hit-and-run about the same time as Jack was firing this kiln load. After Lilly Ann's death, he smashed every piece. He was so angry that the driver was never caught. We both were."

Leslie dabbed her eyes with a dishcloth. Molly looked down at the table, not knowing how to console her hostess. "I didn't mean to upset you. I thought you might want it back. I'm very sorry."

Molly was sure Leslie would ask how Molly had come by the rabbit, but she looked out the window and noticed people clustering around the food table.

"Oh," she sniffed and covered up the rabbit with the box lid, "they're eating already. I'd better go see if everything is out on the table. Do you mind waiting here for a moment?"

"Of course not," Molly answered, feeling terrible.

As Leslie left, Jack Junior entered.

"Where's Ma?" he asked, looking around the room.

"She went outside to check the food."

"Oh good, then I can have a soda," he pronounced, giving himself permission. He opened up the fridge and brought a liter bottle over to Molly.

"Can you get the top off?" he asked her.

Molly opened the bottle and poured him some soda into a small paper cup on the counter. "Don't tell on me," she warned him with a small smile. He promised and then dashed off before his mother returned.

Replacing the cap, Molly returned the bottle to the

fridge. A colorful lunch box caught her eye. Stuffed way back on the bottom shelf, it was an old, metal one, not one of the insulated plastic marvels lacking any trace of personality. And it was a Miss Piggy lunch box, a character from a kid's television show that Molly had always loved.

Without thinking, she reached back behind the loaf of bread and pulled it out. As she opened the latch she realized too late that she held the box upside down. Little glass jars with a clear liquid inside rolled over the kitchen floor.

Molly quickly scooped up the jars and began arranging them inside the lunch box. The label on the back of one caught her eye. It was a prescription in Lilly Ann's name. The jars were filled with insulin.

Molly sat back on her heels, her mind whirling. She had been right about the killer after all. She didn't hear Leslie approach until she was just outside the door, scolding Jack Junior in low tones, which were muffled by the background noise of the celebrating crowd. Molly suddenly recognized the voice.

"Sorry to keep you wait—" Leslie froze as she saw Molly with her daughter's lunch box. She took it from Molly's hands as if it were a wounded bird and closed the lid. Looking at Molly, Leslie realized that she had already guessed the truth.

"I've cleaned out all her things," she began, "but this. This is my old lunch box. It's been sitting in there for two years now. Jack has asked me so many times to take it away, but I just couldn't."

Silently, Molly handed her the last jar of insulin from the floor. Leslie looked at it sorrowfully. "We used to get automatic shipments from a prescription service in Canada. Of course we cancelled it after the accident, but a few weeks ago another one came. Must have been some computer glitch. *I* saw it as a sign. I thought I was done being angry"— she wiped away the tears the had begun to trickle down her freckled cheeks—"but when I saw him again at C. C.'s I knew that I hadn't forgiven and could never forget. I didn't mean to kill him, I swear. I just wanted to make him sick, to make him as miserable as I have been."

"So you knew George-Bradley was a diabetic?" Molly asked softly.

"Yes. He used to come over here frequently, sniffing around for special deals from Jack and trying to flirt with me. I had always disliked the man, but then he stopped coming. He knew that I knew he had killed our daughter."

"He *was* the driver?" Molly asked gently.

Leslie sagged. "No hard proof, of course. He came over with Bunny a few days after the funeral, but he was acting funny. Wouldn't look either of us in the eye and then stole off into the woods, looking behind his shoulder the whole time. I followed him." She took a deep breath. "I had a pair of Lilly Ann's binoculars—she loved to look out for deer or rabbits—and saw him at the accident site. He was looking for something by the road that I had already found."

"What was it?"

"A handkerchief. One of those fancy ones with his initials on it. I took it to the police, but they said it proved nothing. His car was clean and he owns some land down this way, so it didn't prove anything."

Molly remembered how George-Bradley had dabbed his sweaty brow with just such a handkerchief at C. C.'s kiln opening.

Leslie gripped the lunch box until her knuckles turned white. "I think he was in someone else's car, but I know he hit her. There was a big rain that same afternoon. All the tire tracks were erased. There was no evidence anywhere. But I know the fact that he dropped that handkerchief means that he got out of the car. He got out of the car and saw my baby and drove away again."

Leslie balled her hands into fists and then placed them on her stomach as she released a deep exhalation.

She turned to Molly, her eyes wide and glassy. "Do you know how many times I have pictured that scene in my head? Do you know how many times I have wondered if she was still alive at the moment? Did that awful man hear her last words? Was she scared? Did she hurt a lot?" She paused again, to gather strength. Her lips trembled. "And when he didn't find that handkerchief, he made his way back to Jack's workshop. God knows why, but he stole the only thing that survived from that kiln. He stole my Lilly Ann's last gift from her father."

Molly reached out and pulled the weeping woman into her arms. Together, they cried on the kitchen floor until Leslie finally drew away. Miraculously, the party continued outside and no one entered the house. Moments passed as Leslie composed herself and Molly stared at the floor. Finally, Leslie looked at Molly, her face calm but her eyes remained sorrowful and tired.

"Thank you, thank you for hearing me. I am so sorry for leaving you that awful message. Sam Chance told me about your visit and I got scared." She squeezed Molly's hand. "Now it's like I threatened a friend."

Then she stood, picked up the lunch box, and resolutely put it in the trash can. As she smoothed down her flowery sundress she said calmly, "Our lives are starting over again. My little girl is gone. The man who killed her is gone. Jack is working again. And we have a new life on the way. What kind of life that'll be is up to you now."

The scene of the accident became visible in Molly's mind. Lilly Ann darting out of the woods on her bicycle. George-Bradley with Susan, in her car, fooling around as he drove. The impact. Getting out to see if they had hit a deer. The crumpled bike. The unmoving child.

Their horrible secret had divided George-Bradley from Susan, but she had demanded money after their breakup. She bought a new Mercedes and expensive pottery with his money, all the time threatening to tell if he should cut her off. Accustomed to her new lifestyle, she still wanted her blackmail money after his death. But she didn't go to Bunny's house just for the money. She had also gone there to get ahold of the incriminating letter.

George-Bradley must have confessed his hit-and-run crime in a sealed letter to his wife, only to be read in the event of his death. After torturing her for years with his lies and his lovers, George-Bradley gave his wife one last nasty dig. He made Bunny aware of his terrible crime, and about who had been in the car with him.

That was the piece of information Bunny had whispered in Susan's ear the day of the auction. Foolish Bunny! Then Bunny told Susan that she knew all about the accident. She had left Susan no choice but to come after her for the letter.

George-Bradley had killed Lilly Ann. Now he was dead. Susan had killed Bunny and had also been an accessory to her lover's heinous crime. She was going to spend the rest of her life in jail. The Grahams, who had been through so much pain, were starting to feel the sunlight on their faces again. Work. A new baby. A family made whole.

"I'd better get back to my mother," Molly said, smiling shyly. She looked once more at Leslie's stomach, swollen with new life. "She'll be saving some of your delicious fried chicken for me."

Gratefully, Leslie took Molly's hands and placed the shoe box in them. "This little guy belongs to you now. He's had some bad treatment and could use a little love."

"Thank you. Good luck with everything, Leslie."

The older woman gave her a weak smile. "Please come back and see us. Anytime."

"She let you keep the rabbit?" Clara asked on the ride home, eyeing the shoe box on her daughter's lap.

"Yes." Molly gazed out the widow. It was hard for her to carry on a conversation when her mind was spinning with all she had heard from Leslie. What should she do with the truth? All this time she had played at being a detective, and now that she had confirmed the answers to all the riddles, she wished she were still in the dark.

After a pause, she explained why she had the clay animal. "Leslie said the rabbit brings up bad memories for them." And Molly shared only the details about Jack breaking the pieces of kiln number 43 after Lilly Ann's death.

"I can understand that," Clara said. "I am so glad they are back in the swing of things. Jack's work is better than ever—I hope you got enough pictures—and I hear he is going to have another son around Christmas. How wonderful! Someone to learn the family business. Jack Jr. can't seem to settle down long enough to make a pinch pot. I have never seen such a whirlwind of energy. Have you? Molly?"

After such an emotional day, the vibrations of the car and her mother's prattling proved to be too much. Molly was fast asleep, the shoe box cradled in her arms.

Chapter 17

I have seen many people who have come to understand more about themselves through making things with clay and fire.

—HARRY MEMMOTT, FROM *DISCOVERING POTTERY*

Carl Swanson approached Molly's desk chewing feverishly on a piece of gum. He tossed an envelope at her and cleared his throat. "I've got a great assignment lined up for you. You know that TV show, *Hidden Treasures?*" he asked without expecting a reply. "They've agreed to let you spend a week with them this September while they tape an episode in Richmond."

"That does sound like good material for a piece," she agreed and watched as her boss puffed his chest out.

"'Course it does," he snarled in between chews.

Picking up the envelope she asked, "What's this?"

"Look for yourself," he mumbled. "Mr. MacIntosh wanted to give you a bonus for helping circulation reach an all-time high."

"Oh, thank you!" Molly was delighted. Mr. MacIntosh was the paper's owner.

"Don't thank me," Swanson said, truculently. "If I had

my way, you wouldn't get paid extra just for doing your job."

As he turned to plod back to his office, Molly noticed a patch on his right arm. Good thing she was getting out of town to cover several auctions this summer if her boss was going to quit smoking. If people thought he was a S.O.B. before . . .

She tore open the envelope and was elated to see the equivalent of a month's pay. MacIntosh had been very generous. Molly paused for a moment, feeling the weight of her decision about Leslie's secret cloud her happiness.

Molly had written a short letter to Officer Bennett, explaining that Leslie had given George-Bradley a shot of insulin at C. C.'s kiln opening with the intent of making him ill. Molly also described how George-Bradley had killed Lilly Ann and asked Bennett to look for George-Bradley's confessional letter to Bunny. It was probably somewhere in Susan's house, unless she had had enough time before her arrest to destroy it. Lastly, Molly pleaded with Bennett to go easy on the Grahams, emphasizing Leslie's pregnancy.

It was with shaking hands that Molly had dropped the letter in the mailbox. The truth was a heavy burden, and she did not want to be the one to decide what decisions were to be made in the name of justice.

Afterwards, Molly couldn't possibly interview Jack Graham for her final pottery article, but instead wrote a short piece on his return to the public eye and included several descriptive photos from the kiln opening.

Molly shook all thoughts of secrets and murder out of her head. For the tenth time, she assured herself that she had done the right thing and focused on what to do with her extra money. As an idea bloomed in her mind, she shut down her computer and began packing up for the day.

At that moment, the door to Mark's office opened and a

familiar pair of long legs attached to a slim, female body strode out.

"I can't believe you ditched the party, Mark," Amy Byrd cooed. "I was looking for you all night."

"I'll catch up with Paul to do some guy things," Mark said dismissively then bid her a hasty goodbye. She stood open-mouthed at his brusqueness as he made his way over to Molly's desk.

"Hi. Thought I might take the woman of the hour out for a real date," he said loudly enough for Amy to hear. "How about dinner and a movie?"

A real date! Molly couldn't hide her joy. Was he asking her out just to get rid of Amy? No, she didn't think so. Her normally glowing skin flushed radiant as she accepted. Amy Byrd stormed off in a huff, but neither Mark nor Molly gave her any notice.

"Look." Molly waved her check. "Let me take *you* to dinner. I don't have extra money too often." She told Mark about her surprise bonus.

"You can buy me pizza some other time. You need to treat yourself to something special with that money. You deserve it after the month you've had. Let's see, how about a shopping spree, a day at the spa, a weekend in the Outer Banks . . ."

"Actually, I was thinking of taking a class over at the Arts Center."

Mark smiled and picked up her bag as they headed out to the front door. Outside, sheets of rain fell on the warm ground as steam sprang up from the concrete sidewalks. Mark opened a large golf umbrella and beckoned Molly to join him under its protective cover. "But you're already smarter than all of us," he teased. "What kind of class?"

"The kind that starts Friday." Molly turned a beaming

face up to his and called loudly over the beating rain, "It's called Pottery for Beginners."

Rookie officer Monica Clarke was irritated that she was always assigned the job of fetching and sorting the station's mail. Organizing a stack of letters and catalogues for Officer Bennett, Monica noticed that the current edition of his weekly sports magazine featured swimsuit models instead of football players.

"Men," she muttered, cramming Bennett's mail together in a sloppy pile. If Bennett asked her to get him another cup of coffee she would threaten to sue on grounds of discrimination. Little did Monica know that Officer McLeary, a large, muscular black man, had also fetched coffee for Bennett before he was allowed to work the beat. All the rookies started off doing desk work, and they had all gotten Bennett coffee, regardless of gender.

Monica also wasn't aware of a small envelope addressed in neat handwriting to Officer Bennett from a woman named Molly Appleby. Shoved between the pages of his sports magazine, it was completely hidden from view.

Bennett looked up from behind a tall stack of paperwork as Monica entered the room. He groaned at the sight of his pile of mail and knew he would never be free to take his new bride out for lunch.

He brightened when he shifted through the pile to gaze upon the lithe tan body of a brunette in a tiny white bikini. He gazed furtively at the cover, knowing that his possessive wife would not approve of him ogling other women, even airbrushed ones.

Bennett was just about to settle down to a leisurely viewing of a dozen swimsuit models when he heard the familiar clipping of high-heeled shoes and a perky, bright voice moving through the station's main room.

His wife would reach his office in seconds. In a blind panic, Bennett shoved the magazine into the paper shredder and pressed it firmly down into the biting, metal teeth. As his wife stepped into the office, picnic basket in hand, her fiery red hair and wide smile quickly made Bennett forget all about swimsuit models.

Along with a letter detailing the death of a notorious collector, the models had all become thin, feathery ribbons of scrap paper.

The clay sank into the wheel like an old man dropping into a deep, soft chair. The mouth of the bowl spun into a lop-sided yawn that seemed to mock the young hands upon its smooth, wet body.

The potter placed his hands over the boy's, cupping the bowl until the walls sprang high again. The clay recognized the tie between the two sets of hands and began to respect the strength of their union. Together, they forced it to behave with all the love and firmness of a father.

The door to the shed opened and the potter's wife brought in tall, sweating glasses of lemonade. The potter drank the sugary sunlight and smiled in contentment.

Alone, the small hands held the clay steady for a few more turns of the wheel before the bowl keeled over to one side like a sinking ship. The child looked pleadingly at the potter.

Reshaping the fallen clay into a firm ball, the potter re-

placed it on the wheel. He patted his son on the back and held his shoulders as it began to spin.

"You can make another," he told him gently, his voice filled with pride.

The potter was right. He would make another.

He would make thousands.

A Brief Note on Face Jugs

Faces have been given to ceramic vessels throughout history. From Egyptian canobic jars to English toby mugs, face vessels have appeared across the centuries in a multitude of cultures. Though no one knows for certain *why* the first American face jugs were created, historians do know *where* these fascinating objects began to be produced with regularity.

In the western part of South Carolina, in a region called Edgefield, several potters created face jugs, also referred to as "ugly jugs" during the middle of the nineteenth century. Many of these potters were African Americans. These jugs or bottles were turned in the regular manner, and then decorated with applied eyes and horizontal bits of teeth often made with unglazed porcelain. Over time, the subjects of these clay portraits have been lost to us, creating a sense of mystery around each nameless face vessel with its two eyes, two ears, a nose, a mouth, and rows of teeth. One thing is definitive, however, and that is that no two face jugs are alike.

In the early part of the twentieth century, face jugs were not a common part of the southern potter's bread-and-butter sales. During the 1930s, several North Carolina potters began to produce face vessels to sell, but were still relying on their traditional utilitarian wares to support their families. Eventually, technological advancements allowed for the mass production of ceramic ware, and the individual potter either packed it in or found a new attraction to keep his customers returning. For some potters, this attraction was the face jug. Hoping to appeal to tourists, potters spent a great deal of extra time creating a lifelike face or at least one unique enough to catch the eye of a customer.

In the 1960s and 1970s, more and more southern potters began creating face jugs for the tourist trade. Though especially prolific in North Carolina and Georgia, potters throughout the United States made faces on jugs, cups, pitchers, vases, and a variety of other vessels. In the last few decades, those faces have gotten fancy too. Examples such as the female face, war-painted Native Americans, devils, Medusas, and even animal face vessels have been introduced into the mix. Some potters have also made two-faced jugs, with one side being a devil and the other an angel, a man and a woman, a happy and a sad face, or a two-faced, irreverent representation of the politician.

The face jug has been called "grotesque" in the past and it is true—many *are* a bit daunting with their pointed teeth, bleeding eyes, long fangs, or devil horns. But the face jug is an excellent example of how an art form can be created in a few workshops in one area in the country, and then slowly appear in other regions. For whatever reason that first American face vessel was made, whether for religious or ritualistic purposes, as a gift, or simply as an artistic experiment, the face jug was born to be embraced, over time, by thousands of artists and collectors.

Examples of Southern Face Jugs

CLOCKWISE: Face Jug with orange lead glaze and porcelain chip teeth by NC Folk Potter Billy Ray Hussey; Face Jug with drippy alkaline glaze by Georgia Potters Cleater and Billie Meaders; Devil Jug with matte red glaze and porcelain chip teeth by NC Folk Potter Louis Brown.

COUNTER-CLOCKWISE: Face Jug with alkaline glaze and clay teeth by GA Folk Potter Lanier Meaders; Face Jug with swirl glaze and porcelain chipped teeth by NC Folk Potter Charles Lisk; Face Jug with cobalt highlight and double row of porcelain teeth by NC Folk Potter Archie Teague

The scrapbooking mystery series from
Laura Childs

Carmela Bertrand owns a scrapbooking
store in New Orleans—and can't help but
solve a murder every once in a while.

Keepsake Crimes
0-425-19074-9

Photo Finished
0-425-19434-5

Bound for Murder
0-425-19923-1

Available wherever books are sold or at
penguin.com